and after that

Jaylakshmi Bhattacharya

Gpi
Garev Publishing
International

ISBN 978-0-9707558-6-5

And After That is a work of fiction. Though some characters, incidents and dialogues are based on personal experience, the work as a whole is the product of the author's imagination. All characters in this publication are fictitious and any resemblance to any real person, living or dead is strictly coincidental.

and after that

GAREV PUBLISHING INTERNATIONAL, INC

European address:
50 Highpoint, Heath Road
Weybridge, Surrey KT13 8TP
England

Tel: (44) (0) 1932 844526

Email: garevpi@aol.com

North American address:
1095 Jupiter Park Drive,
Suite 7, Jupiter, FL 33458
USA

Tel: 561 697 1447

Email: garevpub@aol.com

www.garevpublishing.com

Garev Publishing International

- and after that -

PROLOGUE

Maya's vision became increasingly dim and hazy, things getting smaller and smaller until she could no longer see them distinctly. Yet, she tried doing the impossible at seeking the now obscure landscape, which only hurt her eyes and made them water. Not willing to relax her over-strained eyes, Maya continued looking down, as if by doing so, she could catch a glimpse of her past. It was paradoxical that she wanted to see what she was running from, leaving it behind in Calcutta. It seemed that she wanted to relive that particular day when her beloved husband Avik, in a fit of rage, pushed her with all his might before leaving the house and slamming the door behind him. Following the shock of the fall, she felt an excruciating pain in her belly, which was superseded by a warm sticky liquid seeping out of her body. In spite of that, she tried to raise herself from the floor but couldn't. The pain had come again; this time not only from her belly but also from the core of her heart, as she saw the growing patch of blood on her dress. The cramps had come again along with the realization that her unborn child of three months was miscarried prematurely from the warm cozy nook of her womb. The growing pool of blood was all she had seen before falling unconscious. The thought that Avik had done this to her was what she remembered and kept repeating long after regaining her senses and consequently many failed counseling sessions later, and …

"Excuse me madam, would you like a vegetarian or non-vegetarian meal?" asked the airline flight attendant in her well-trained, polite and impersonal voice. Maya was jolted back to the present hearing the voice and looked up to the immaculately made-up face of Tanushree, a hostess on the Indian domestic aircraft on which she was flying. Indeed, the name Tanushree, as pinned on the lapel of her dress, complimented the perfect figure she had, mused Maya. However, she registered all these details slowly, as her mind struggled out of the deep ocean of her memories. Taken slightly aback, she responded: "What? Oh, yes, make it non-vegetarian, please" and she turned back to look through the window to catch one last glimpse of the contours of her beloved city with all its variegated splendor some twenty to thirty thousand feet below the small plane from where she sat.

PART I

Contemplating that horrible day always reminded Maya of the domestic help she had at home; a woman used to come everyday to assist her with the household work and that fateful day was no exception. Appearing as accustomed, she found Maya alone lying unconscious on the floor. With the subsequent gentle nursing of her neighbors, brought together by Mina, her maid, Maya's senses were restored. Maya remembered the warmth of Mina with fondness akin to love; she was small and stout with a dark complexion, her sari was worn with military precision and an air of total efficiency, in contrast to her ever ready collection of juicy local gossip. She also remembered how Mina was a part of her life when she was newly wed and learned the ropes of running a household. She had been a part of Maya's newly acquired status of married woman that was accentuated by the accessories of Hindu marriage: Sankha (white bangle of conch shell), Pola (Red Bangle) and Sindur (Vermillion dust worn on the forehead and hair parting as a sign of marriage). Mina had been witness to Maya's learning, such as answering to the call of boudi (sister-in-law), a mark of love and respect as it is customary in Bengal when addressing a married woman; whether she is addressed by folks on the bus, at shops, on the streets and by the Bengali world at large.

Beaz, Maya's childhood friend whose real name was Bipasha, had been almost sarcastic when she laughed and asked Maya, "Responsibility, what kind can there be when it's just the two of you? Man, I would have freaked out. Imagine candlelit dinners, loud music, dancing, sometimes with friends sometimes just the two of us; watching really cool videos, eating strawberry with champagne, going out and coming in whenever it suited us, partying and, of course, sex. The glorious gorgeous sex – anytime, every time, anywhere, everywhere! On the sofa, on the dinner table, kitchen floor... Gosh, the list is endless!" "Really, must you always boil everything down to sex?" Maya asked. "One would think the basic purpose of the institution of marriage was to give you the license to kill yourself with an overdose of sex", said Maya, beginning to get annoyed, for it was never possible to speak about anything serious with Beaz without ending up talking about sex. It also reminded Maya of those endless phone talks with Beaz during their high school days when they would exchange the various dirty stories circulated at school.

In retrospect, mused Maya, how mandatory it was, to hold such discourses at the end of each day. Almost every day they had some sexy topic to discuss as both had respective sets of friends from different sections to supply the sexual manure to their overly fertile minds. "But things are different now, aren't they?" questioned Maya. Really gone were those carefree days of sauntering through the college campus, when their discussion had lost the spurt of the overcharged hormonal activities of their adolescent years. Although the topic had remained the same over the years, there were major changes, the variation being the list of male admirers, boyfriends and sugar daddies over innumerable cups of tea. There were four of us, reminisced Maya, who would invade the university cafeteria table number five and keep it as the forum for long discourses, drinking tea in small, much used and much less washed, white cups with saucers left with barely visible and faded pink floral prints that struggled to remain seen. Even the chipped edges of the cups, which are the harbinger of many small and big water borne diseases, did not seem to deter us from the ritual of holding court in the canteen at table number five, day in and day out.

 After the short lunch, which was returned half eaten, Maya felt too restless to take a nap or read the in-flight magazine that had an inviting front page cover. So she checked her watch instead, to see how much of her flight was left. The steely hands of the watch pointed to 9:45 p.m., which meant about forty-five minutes before arrival. Bored and with nothing else to do, she turned her thoughts to her honeymoon brooding over how quickly that phase of her marriage had gone and how the wristwatch was the last of the gifts from Avik. Fumbling with the seat belt, unsure whether to put it on at that moment or later, Maya decided to freshen up. Taking out the mirror and her favorite mocha lipstick from her handbag, she peered into the mirror, applied it and checked the effect. A touch of eyeliner, a dash of lipstick was all she wanted to apply; but she couldn't help noticing the lines of tension and pain around the corners of her eyes, a warning sign of fleeting youth for all women. Even though Maya didn't consider herself vain, she felt these lines, if left unattended would surely turn into wrinkles on her otherwise flawless skin. She was always proud of her skin and her wheat-colored complexion with its natural and healthy glow, like a smooth, even suntan acquired at an exorbitant charge in an exotic location. She could always pretend to belong to that rich, alien breed with whom she associated in her fantasies. White sandy beaches, palm trees and hammocks, relaxing in the sparkling blue water lapping against her body, or lying under a colorful umbrella on a chaise longue with a striped blue and white towel, sipping some exotic, non-alcoholic drink. She envisioned a red, wide headband holding her hair from flying in all directions and adding to her sex appeal, a glorious mix of the latest bikini, complete with a silky sarong. Last but not least, she pictured a strong, handsome man catering to her.

Of course, the seeds of such rich and colorful fantasies found their origin in the glossy pages of the magazines that she managed to sneak into her room in the quiet, darkness of the night, away from the prying eyes of her parents. She also hid her fantasies from her brother Nikhil, as he always threatened to tell her parents. Just a year and a half younger, Nikhil had always been nosey and demanded attention from their parents. It was he who was the actual menace to her and her close friends and their collection of magazines, and romantic, sexy paperbacks. One day, he almost caught her wearing a sexy bra, preening in front of the mirror with Beaz sitting on the bed and critically examining the effect. The door was not properly closed and during his eavesdropping and peeping spree, he tripped on the rug outside and stumbled into the room. He was received with utter disgust, loud protests and a resounding smack on his cheek. The near fiasco of him running to mother to babble out everything was stalled with a promise of a few posters of his favorite sportsmen. Maya laughed aloud and thought it was odd that while memories can be quite taxing on a peaceful state of mind, like her present state, post the divorce, they can also come as relief, like rain to a parched land after a very traumatic drought. It made her laugh and think of her brother with a strong pull in her heart, which she never experienced before –never realizing that the brother she had thought a menace

- and after that -

during their growing years, held such a large spot in her heart. Men are strange about ways they discover the fundamentals of life, of relationships and even about themselves, thought Maya.

The voice of the captain over the microphone broke her reverie, as he said:

"This is Captain Sharma speaking, we have reached Bangalore. The outside temperature is 29 degrees Celsius. I hope you had a pleasant flight and we look forward to having you fly with us again, thank you". The speaker clicked off and the sign for the seat belt clicked on as the plane readied itself for touch down. She began readjusting her lemon yellow georgette sari, shaking out the creases, then Maya's eyes glanced down at her chest and she focused on the inch-sized idol of Lord Ganesha[1] around her neck with a single diamond between the eyes; a gift from Nikhil on her last birthday. He had sent it to her from Mumbai because he knew that over the years she had become a devotee of Lord Ganesha. In fact, it was quite a while since she had seen Nikhil and his sweet funny wife, Neeta, thought Maya. That's the trouble when you have a baby, an uncompromising job and a fast and expensive life to maintain, justified Maya. Well, she will have to do some social rounds in the near future, but not now. Now she is running away from it all.

While Ganesha nested cozily in her cleavage, she carried on with the critical examination of her physical attributes and thought for a woman of 5 feet 5 inches, breasts of 34C seemed a little too wanting with a hip line of 40. It was this padding at the lower end, which prompted her to take to saris since her university days. While, Beaz and her other friends would be experimenting with the tightest of dresses and jeans, Maya would make an exception from time to time

[1]Ganesha is the elephant-deity who is one of the best-known and most worshipped deities in Hinduism. He is the Lord of success and destroyer of evils and obstacles. He is the patron of arts and sciences, and the god of intellect and wisdom.

with churidar and salwar suits, the authentic Indian dresses. The other carry-over from her university days was the waist-length, slightly wavy, brownish-black hair that she kept severely tied back in a single long monotonous braid. Today was no exception. Her otherwise light brown eyes, always twinkling with laughter and wit, stared back at her, unsure from the depth of her compact mirror. The long thick lashes from under well-shaped brows did not seem to give her the much needed confidence that her usual, striking intelligent look used to convey. Her sharp chin pointed in defiance to her current situation and her soft, full and voluminous lips quivered a little. However, with an effort she pulled herself together and concentrated on getting off the plane. Maya was just beginning to dial her friend's number when she caught her waving and coming towards her from the parking lot.

"Priya, thank God you made it" exclaimed Maya. "I was really beginning to think…" continued Maya but Priya interrupted her

"Tense as usual, when will you learn to relax? I know you are under stress but remember it's me you are going to stay with now and not some boorish and insensible man. Besides, I managed to get the office car at this time so I could pick you up" said Priya.

Maya looked fondly at Priya and felt a sense of security and inspiration flow back into her body. Priya had always been like this, confident and pragmatic. She was always busy, trying out new things for Maya and in turn forcing some of these things onto others in their group. Maya mused and smiled. Undoubtedly, Maya needed a push in order to do things was Priya's verdict on her dear friend. With a smile on her face, Maya began to relax as she leaned into the leather-upholstered comfortable car. Her enthusiastic friend on the other hand, started pointing at landmarks of the city, which had become her home in the past three years. Shapes and sizes of silhouettes zoomed by them in the dark, as did the names of the places, which Priya kept rattling on, Hennur Road, Leela Palace Hotel, Lingarajapuram, Ulsoor Lake M.G. Road, Brigade Road… they all sounded like a recital of phonetics to Maya's ear but she did not mind at all. In fact, she even tried to give the impression she understood and registered everything being uttered by Priya. Although she was happy to see her friend again, she kept hiding her yawns and pretended to be interested in what Priya had to say. After experiencing her first unescorted flight, the fear of the unknown slowly began ebbing out of her. A mix of emotions crept up her body, not even tiredness refrain her from feeling the intermittent nicks of excitement like bug bites.

"You know Priya, I have really missed you and wanted to get in touch with…sort of to revive that wonderful friendship we shared before." Maya said somberly.

"I know, but you were too lazy to even return my call when I invited you to my party. In fact, I was so hurt that you, of all people would not come to the party I had organized. I was very disappointed and thought you did not care for me as much as I did for you." exclaimed Priya.

"I know dear, in fact, I hated myself for realizing it too late. I felt so miserable thinking that I had lost you. I did not even call you the next day, and by the time I did…"

"The bird had flown the cage," purred Priya showing satisfaction.

"Yes, but I am grateful to God that by either serendipity or fate I ran into our common friend Ranjita at the shopping mall. She gave me your address and told me everything about you, including the break up. I was stunned and felt terribly sorry …."

"Maybe the ring was not reason enough to keep me tied to the sacred institution of marriage. Maybe I counted my chickens before they hatched. Or perhaps long years of married life were not for me. It may not have suited me in the long run. Who knows?" she said and looked out the window, but not before Maya caught a glimpse of her moist eyes.

"Priya dear, does it still hurt even after two years?" asked Maya with deep concern. "Yes, it does, even after I broke up with the last guy" said Priya.

Fourteen days had passed and Maya was starting to get frustrated with the classified columns. It seemed that her urgent need to be independent was getting forever delayed. Her Master's Degree in Zoology was not what employers were looking for in a job candidate. Another disqualifying factor was her lack of any professional experience. Career-wise she had no skills in any kind of job, except that of running a household all by herself, playing the efficient role of a cook, keeper of the house and wife. Was she at fault for being an amateur? It felt like playing a game of darts where you consistently come close to the bull's eye but never hit it. Sometimes her age seemed to pose a problem. She was always outside the stipulated age criteria: sometimes only by a few years, sometimes too far off for her to even consider going to the interview. Since she never belonged to the labor force, she lacked the knowledge of what a base salary was. Additionally, the fact that she was not in her early twenties anymore didn't help. Was she at fault for being 29? Well, she knew she was late again. She's always been late for everything, starting with her birth. She was behind schedule coming out of her mother's womb. Her mother's contractions were not strong enough to expel her so the doctor intervened, prodding with forceps to get her out. She was delayed taking her first baby steps. She was the last one to fall in love among her high school friends. She was late starting her career and of course, she was the last one to get married. However, she had made amends for all the other adversities when she dissolved her marriage of three years in an abrupt and decisive way. Although, she refused to take full credit for her failed marriage since Avik, her husband was mostly responsible for it. He nurtured their marriage with his aloofness and neglect. Their relationship was characterized by sudden, senseless fights with tirades of meaningless words followed by silence. Hours passed, sometimes days, and silence had taken over their house until it became totally unbearable for her. She craved for a single gaze, a simple smile or anything that would indicate a truce. Instead, Avik's loathsome look pierced Maya's heart like the venomous sting of a scorpion. She waited in vain for a sign that never came. It was always up to her to mend the broken bridge between them, to find peace, to make a livable environment for their sake. This led her to the idea that a child could do wonders for what was left of the relationship. Knowing how Avik would react to the news of having a baby, she decided to hide her scheme from him. One fateful night, she managed to seduce Avik and assured him she practiced the rhythm method, which is a way to prevent pregnancy by not having sex around the time of ovulation. To Maya's advantage, they hadn't had sex in weeks so her wheat-colored complexion turned desirable and her breasts had suddenly become an aphrodisiac for Avik. Crazed by lust, he gave in to his animal instinct and didn't hear what Maya had said. It was too late for him to retract now. That night she conceived.

Morning sickness, fatigue, drowsiness and uncontrollable appetite revealed Maya's condition. Avik confronted her to clear his doubts; he feared her answer. Maya couldn't hide it anymore and told him she was pregnant. She tried to explain but his face reddened and let a scream escape his mouth. "How, when, why?" yelled Avik and continued ranting "How in God's name am I going to manage this situation?" He closed his fists, lifted his right hand and denounced "You tricked me!" He went on with his outburst saying he couldn't support his parents, her and the baby and demanded she get a job. He was condescending, cruel and spiteful in his words. Maya was deeply hurt but the thought she was going to be a mother gave her strength. She looked forward to her pregnancy and pictured herself nursing her little one from her bosom. She would devote herself entirely to the baby and provide all the love the father would deny. Unfortunately, Maya's dream was shattered and her baby's life cut short by Avik's selfish act. An accident as Maya described it was just her way of denying the truth. The emptiness in her eyes depicted hopelessness, and crying had become as natural as breathing in the last eight months. Sometimes she didn't even know that she was crying until she felt a tightening sensation followed by a slight burning in her eyes. She found herself absentminded most of the time with her thoughts sailing aimlessly.

Living in Bangalore with Priya for the last two weeks helped her indeed heal her wounds. She spent a lot of time with Priya and observed her friend's resilience through the vicissitudes of life. She learned a lot from her friend's way of coping with pain and heartaches. Suddenly, her perspective on her share of problems didn't seem as overwhelming as she once thought they were. She promised

- and after that -

herself to be stronger and was willing not to give up before trying, as she usually did. If there was something to be learned from other people ... well, Priya had lots to offer. Her tenacity to plod under the weight of a burden, almost ruthless, was admirable. She accepted challenges and refused to give up on life. She handled the breaking of her engagement undauntedly. Unfortunately, Maya had not been there to console her friend. Instead, she heard it in detail from Ranjita. Maya learned the facts; ten days before the wedding, the guy got cold feet, he was afraid of such serious commitment. The invitations were already printed, the reservation at the hall was paid for, the menu was planned out and all the minor details had been taken care of. It was a disaster indeed for Priya's family. The shame, embarrassment, and the agony of seeing their only daughter being humiliated in this way was too much to bear for her father that came close to having a heart attack. Now it was almost impossible to recognize that softhearted girl that she had known in her university days. Reality had gripped Priya so tightly that the acquired veneer of practicality, optimism and invincibility replaced the old Priya almost completely.

The polyphonic ring tones of the cellular phone broke Maya's reverie and she jumped up startlingly; she felt guilty because instead of getting ready for dinner she had been daydreaming. Actually, wallowing in self-pity, as Priya had said time and again. In fact, she had just remembered as the phone rang she had evening plans. She had been drifting in irreparable memories.

"Hello" said Maya.

"Are you ready? The car is on its way. It should be there in the next 20-30 minutes" said Priya.

"Actually I have ..." began Maya but was cut short by Priya.

"Don't tell me you forgot, and you can't decide what to wear. You don't have time for all that" said Priya.

"I really don't feel like going, plus I have nothing decent to wear" Maya almost pleaded.

"Well, then come in your basic for-all-I-care outfit, but come! You must. This will be my third attempt to get you out to socialize. Third time is the charm, right? So just get dressed, ok?" said Priya.

"Yeah, but …" started Maya.

"Thirty minutes … see you at The Taste of China!" said Priya and hung up the phone. Maya was in a tight spot. First, she had to decide on a dress, then she had to pay attention to make-up and hair and most importantly work on her mood. She definitely needed to do something regarding this issue; her semblance needed to be cheerful and appealing, which she lacked these days. Although she knew she couldn't conceal her true feelings, she had the option to do something about her appearance. She decided to mask her sad eyes with a lot of make-up to deter people from digging out the truth that ripped her heart. Perhaps, if she colored her lips in a luscious red it would draw a fake smile, Maya thought. It was this expressive face that helped her win many trophies in the inter-college contests as she enacted different roles and characters with ease. Her college professors were proud of her and were sure that one day Maya Ghosal would turn out to be a great performer or television personality. But what Maya turned out to be was even surprising to her. In spite of all those years of great performances, Maya felt oddly nervous about going out to socialize. She didn't feel comfortably playing the role of herself. Her numbness didn't allow her to be a gregarious being.

As the hotel manager showed her the table of Ms. Priya Mishra and her friends, Maya tried her best not to trip over or slip in her current state of excitement and nervousness. She still couldn't believe she was attending a social event after so long. She was about to pull the loose end of her powdery chiffon sari around her shoulder when she realized that today was done more tightly than in her customary way, as it was pinned to her left shoulder and not left hanging. Also unlike other days, she was wearing a single string of pink pearl necklace and a set of pink pearl drop earrings. On her right wrist she wore a string wristlet of pearls. A simple steel band oval watch with a mother of pearl dial adorned her left wrist. She made sure to leave her hair loose today, which hugged her face gently and the slight waves softened the cheekbones giving her features a more oval look.

"Hi Maya, I'm glad that you did not keep us waiting any longer" said Priya with a smile indicating the chair on her left and turning to the man sitting on the right. "First, let me get the introductions out of the way because I have news to share. This is Dhiraj, my friend here has his own business and travels a lot, always on the go, his business deals with gadgets. This is Rita, she works with me in Jet Airways whom you have met before and next to her is Aakash. He is a friend of Rita's and a big fish in the film industry, he makes all kinds of movies, and finally, meet Gaurav friend of both." Maya was nodding with an ephemeral smile as she was being introduced from one person to the next in quick succession, but paused at Rita to say

"Hi, how are you?"

"Fine sweetie, so how are things with you?" asked Rita.

"Just about alright" said Maya.

"Well, now that Maya is also here looking cute as a button, I have a toast to make. Dhiraj and I" Priya paused, she raised her glass and resumed to say "… are going to tie the knot in late December!" She grinned.

"What?" Rita exclaimed gulping down her drink and Maya opened her eyes wide tilting her head as in perplexity.

"Late December Priya? December is just around the corner. With your shopping, my shopping for the occasion, planning a leave, lord it's too tight" wailed Rita.

"Actually it's never too soon to get married to the person you love. But I agree with Rita. It was quite a surprise, a pleasant one, but I simply can't imagine how you kept such secret though," said Maya still with a puzzled look on her face.

"And I thought we were more than colleagues, I thought we were close friends and you still manage to keep this from me. Ok, enough, I'm glad for you guys" said Rita kissing Priya, and then she shook Dhiraj's hand.

"My heartfelt congratulations to you both" said Maya in a sweet voice. Priya was really glowing or at least that's what it looked like to Maya. In fact, for the past two days Priya had looked radiant, cheerful, and with a permanent smile on her face. Maya had noticed her demeanor but concluded that it was due to the deal of the merger going on at work. Being a Public Relations Manager wasn't an easy job. Priya had to stay on top of everything if she wanted to beat the stiff competition. Staying in business these days seemed an accomplishment in itself and to actually do well it required more than just a university degree, it required skills.

"Now, if we are allowed to have a say in the matter and you nice ladies permit, we would love to say something, what do you say Aakash?" said Gaurav and continued with his speech. "What does a

- and after that -

man have to say to his buddy at a time like this? Except, congrats ...
let's have a drink!" Gaurav raised his glass and swung it in the air.
The rest of the group followed and drank in their honor.

"Ok, it's true we girls have more to say, but that's just because we
always say the right things. Right Priya?" Rita said with a smug look.

"Well, to begin with, I am honored to be a part of this special
evening. Congratulations to both of you! It's been quite a while since
I last saw such a perfect couple excited about their future. It's one of
the most engaging and wonderful sights" said Aakash in his deep
voice. Maya tried to pay attention to what Aakash was saying without
looking directly at him. Oddly, she felt shy and extremely conscious
of him. It was not so much his unconventional good looks but
something about his personality almost ethereal that made him
interesting. Before they ordered they continued talking and voices
mingled while discussing the menu. Everybody had something to say
about almost everything, but like Maya, Aakash had very little to say.
She rationalized further, that while she was tongue-tied because of
her recent traumatic past; his silence seemed deliberate and
measured. Yet, she could not feel at ease to start a conversation with
him. The round table gave everybody a perfect angle to see and listen
to each other. The oriental décor, dim lights and typical oriental
music, predominantly of flute, cast the most romantic spell to the
place. Maya felt a thrill being surrounded by new people, in a new
place, away from everything that was known to her as home. A
sudden desire to start her life all over filled her existence. Suddenly,
Aakash called for a second toast. "I would like to propose another
toast ... this time to myself as I also have something to share ..."

"You too?" Rita shouted excitedly interrupting Aakash. "Now this is too much, two surprises and I had no clue! It's really unthinkable!"

"Come on Rita, let Aakash give his news first, I am in such high spirits to be kept waiting any longer" said Priya.

"Actually, I knew about it and I could have told you guys, but I didn't want to be a killjoy. It's his story; he should do the honors" said Gaurav and winked at Rita. "Gauraaaav" Rita practically screamed. Maya prayed silently for Rita to stop and let Aakash begin his recital in that deep voice of his, which was beginning to sound soothing, comforting almost hypnotic to her. In her excitement and anticipation she tugged her sari, which was already in its proper place, out of sheer habit with the intention of drawing it close to her. But to her utter dismay the safety pin came off with a quick abandon and flew off in Aakash's direction. Instantly, the end of her powdery chiffon sari neatly folded all this time released itself from the folds covering half of her left arm, falling close to her champagne glass. It would have bared her completely if Aakash had not intervened. Just before it went too far, he said "May I?" and caught the runaway sari-end and deposited it in her shaky hand. Blushing deeply, she managed to look at him and murmur a soft "Thank you." She lowered her head not daring to look at the other faces at the table. Fear and embarrassment made her imagine that she was a spectacle to everyone around her including the chefs. Thankfully, it was only her over-wrought imagination at its worst! When she worked up the courage to look at him she was rather surprised at the expression on Aakash's face, more specifically his eyes. There was no mocking gleam or sexual connotation of any kind in that look. In lieu, there was a deep concern for her, camouflaged by anger. It was a look that was strangely intimate considering this was their first meeting, and it seemed to reprimand her silently for her inability to take care of her sari … of herself. Maya excused herself and took a quick trip to the ladies room. Upon her return, everybody waited for Maya to sit down so Aakash could resume his speech.

"Well as I was saying, this morning I got a call from my editor advising me that our last documentary has been approved by The National Geographic Channel."

"Hey, that's cool! What's the topic? "Priya said.

"I knew what the first one was about, what's this one on?" asked Rita.

"Yeah, I remember that documentary. It was well done. It was about the NGOs[2] in Calcutta and the immense work they are doing" said Dhiraj appreciatively.

"When was this? Anyway, tell us about the new one Aakash. When is it due? I want to watch this one" said Priya.

"Guys, enough with all these questions and comments, doesn't he deserve more than a toast for such great news?" asked Gaurav. "Instead, we could have a blast at the new nightclub that opened up on Church Street, off Brigade Road." Added Gaurav. "That's a great idea! We could all meet on Saturday provided Aakash it's ok with it" said Dhiraj. Maya thought it was a bit insensitive on their part. A little selfish if someone asked her. How could they show no concern for his feelings, no desire to know what his documentary was about?

"Why aren't you saying anything? Are you not interested in joining them?" Aakash's voice intruded Maya's thoughts. Maya looked at him and wanted to say what she was thinking, how sad she felt these people who called themselves his friends were not at all interested in listening about his project. She wanted to tell him never mind

[2]Representatives of independent citizen organizations known at the UN as Non-Governmental Organizations who are often the most effective voices for the concerns of ordinary people in the international arena.

them…I will listen. She was speechless and all bashful Maya was able to do was stare at him. Before Maya had a chance to utter a word, Priya jumped in and said

"What is she going to say? Don't you know Maya has denounced mankind and its worldly affairs? At the ripe age of 29 she has decided to call it quits, and dedicate her days to denying the pleasures of life. I intend to throw a party in her honor for being so brave and finally deciding to go out with us today."

"Good then, we will have twice the reasons to celebrate at the nightclub" said Gaurav and looked enquiringly at Maya.

"But I don't like nightclubs" said Maya apprehensively fearing another outburst from her friend. Lifting her hands into the air with a gesture of despair Priya announced to her friends she was right. "There, see what I was talking about?"

"Come on Maya, you will like it! I promise you" said Rita. Smiling a little Maya said "I am a total misfit there; I have tried it before, it was a total failure."

"Maya, you really need to lighten up" declared Priya.

"Oh Priya, give her a break, I know what she means" Aakash said. "We can do something else instead."

"Like what?" interrupted Dhiraj, who had been quiet all this time watching this play of words with interest.

"Like coming to my house, it could be a small but intimate rendezvous." Aakash then looked straight at Maya and said, "I think you will like that." She let out a sigh of relief knowing she didn't have to comply with their decision. But she was taken aback by his suggestion. Maya looked at Aakash and said "Yes that will be better." So it was decided that they wouldn't go the nightclub and instead organize a small gathering at Aakash's place one of these days.

It was the third time in the evening that Maya got up to drink water and relieve herself. She carried this pattern since her college days when she couldn't get any sleep due to nervousness fretting about the next day's exam. Normally a sound sleeper but a situational insomniac- was her very own diagnosis. Finally, overwhelmed with fatigue from getting up so many times and being unable to sleep she decided to watch television instead. In the cozy little bungalow where Priya stayed, the living room was in the middle with one bedroom on each side with their respective bathrooms, followed by the kitchen at the end of the hallway. Quietly, without turning on the main light, Maya switched on the bedside lamp, came out to the living room and turned on the television. Switching channels listlessly was no help either, she realized. She went back to bed to try to get some sleep. She needed to be rested because the next day would be an important day for Maya, a promising one perhaps. Priya found Maya sleeping peacefully on her side. Her long wavy hair resembled a velvety veil as if protecting her fragile state. Priya felt loving-kindness towards her dear friend, like the one a mother offers to her child but she also felt pity for everything she had gone through in Calcutta. She sincerely hoped that this interview worked out. Priya knew that Maya needed no financial assistance to support herself, as she had enough savings. But this job would help Maya recover her lost self-confidence and her sense of worth. Divorce is never easy, but in Indian society divorced individuals carry disrepute, a stigma that follows them everywhere! Thus, restarting one's life was a difficult task indeed. Self-esteem and reliance took a back seat. Going through a broken engagement had taught Priya this.

"Maya aren't you going to your interview?" asked Priya, gently shaking her and pulling off the cover.

"Hmmm" was the only response that greeted Priya.

"Maya, wake up! I am going to be late too. Maya!" said Priya loudly.

"What?" Maya asked, and looked at Priya with unfocused eyes. She moaned and stretched her arms above her head, grabbed the watch lying on the nightstand and muttered "Oh, no! It's eight thirty already? My interview is at ten o'clock, what shall I do now? How am I going to get there on time?" Maya panicked.

"Well? Just get up! Have your tea and start your day. I'm off, I can't wait anymore. All the best for your interview, keep your calm, ok?" said Priya and hugged her. The fresh smell of Priya's skin blended with talcum and her favorite French perfume wafted to Maya's nose. She hugged Priya back. Priya then got her handbag, took a hurried sip from her cup of tea and waved at Maya closing the door behind her. Meanwhile, Maya was mentally organizing a schedule of her day. She wondered if she had time to practice her interview in front of the mirror. She always felt confident if she rehearsed this scenario beforehand. This exercise was something she had read in a self-help book, one of many life-changing books by authors who promised to help rid of all your bad habits, make you an exceptional human being, a successful entrepreneur, make you rich and prosperous or make your body the epitome of good health in record-breaking time. But Maya never had the chance to practice any of this or even remember it at a time of crisis! Today, however she remembered a chapter on creative visualization so she pictured herself going to this interview and coming out with a big smile and a secured job. Maya had a good feeling about this interview so she wasted no time and put into practice what she had read in the books. She was brilliant just like her good old stage days at the university theatre.

Maya's first non- professional meeting, which turned out to be as equally nerve wrecking as a job interview, was when she met Avik's parents. He was the only son of a well-off family whose father held a respectable government position. His mother was a homemaker who always made sure to keep the house worthy of a dignitary. Last but not least, his two sisters, one married and one betrothed, were exemplary society girls. Avik's mother was no dignitary at all, but her overbearing personality could have made her one. She was treated with deepest respect by her children and her orders were carried out efficiently. Although, she was a very devout woman she had not been able to extricate herself from the clutches of superstitions, myths and everlasting charms and powers of the sadhus[3] and fortune- tellers. That's why Avik's mother was infuriated when she learned her son had chosen a girl without consulting her or a fortune-teller. "So, you are the girl, huh?" asked his mother when Maya bent down to touch her feet as was the usual custom still followed strictly nowadays. "Yes" said Maya and smiled broadly as she usually did. "I see" was all she said. Her smile was not returned. Instead, she saw statue-like faces with prying eyes from all members of his family. Perhaps she was not suitable to be part of the Sanyal clan. After spending just one lengthy hour and having two sweetmeats, she realized that her life was going to be very difficult indeed. In reality, starting a new life next to the man she loved didn't scare Maya what she feared the most was her new family. In Asian countries, mostly in India the girls are groomed from a tender age to be ready to be good wives. A girl grows up with her biological family only to go to her sasural or in-laws, once

[3]A Sadhu is a Hindu ascetic or monk. It consists of renouncing worldly ties in pursuit of higher values of life.

27

she is married. All her future actions from then onward would be the moral and social duty of the husband, and the mother-in-law would be second in command. On the other hand, their western counterparts are encouraged to be independent, and learn to be their husband's equals. Even though, this picture is myopic in some parts of India, there is an emerging enlightenment in other parts of the country. But again, the emancipating light had missed the Sanyal family completely.

Nevertheless, the wedding took place and Maya began her new life as the wife of Avik Sanyal. A few months passed by and the constant taunts, complaints and disrespect by her in-laws formed part of Maya's married life. Maya was naïve to think this situation would improve with time. On the contrary, it went too far. There was no way of pleasing her mother-in-law. So without saying anything, Avik and Maya finally moved out.

Auto rickshaw or auto as is commonly known in India, is one of the chief modes of transport in Bangalore, —it is a small two- or three-wheeled motorized version of the traditional rickshaw and one of the most popular means of public transportation in urban India— so getting one in the city was no problem. "Brigade Towers, please" Maya told the driver. "Which way?" The driver asked "Any way, just find a short cut, please." "Woke madam, woke" said the driver shaking his head side to side in a typically Southern Indian manner, even pronouncing the word "ok" with "W" instead of "O". However, tense as she was, today she didn't find this humorous and concentrated on the interview ahead. Strangely enough Maya felt both nervous and excited about the imminent interview. She thought this could be her chance to start all over again since she found this job by pure coincidence. Earlier that week she had been going through the pages of the Bangalore Times classified ads and happened to spot this brief advertisement:

"Teachers needed to teach foreign students.

Contact over the phone."

Intrigued, she called up the number and discovered it was a special program created within the college, which in turn was affiliated to Bangalore University looking for English professors to teach students from Iran. She could not imagine the tremendous task involved and the experience required for it. Teaching English to Indian students as opposed to Iranians, as she found out later, was completely different. English, though technically a foreign language has become some sort of adopted language in India. There are instances in which Indians use more English words in a sentence than their mother tongue. Equally prevalent is the practice to pepper the mother tongue with English words. One can hear it everywhere; thoughts get better translated in it. Children get used to it since they hear this at home, in school, on TV, and sometimes even mothers coo to them in English. But what did this mean to an Iranian? Mused Maya seriously. She was expecting the Director's Assistant to say "No, thank you for calling" since she mentioned to her she had a Master's Degree in Zoology, not English. Surprisingly, that had not been the case. On the contrary, she was fascinated by her well-rounded curriculum and advised her she had a good chance. It was on her persistence that Maya was heading towards the Global English Center today.

Maya arrived a few minutes early and announced herself to the receptionist. She sat down and waited for the director. There were two other teachers waiting for their turn to be interviewed. They were middle-aged with a rather serious expression on their face. This made Maya a little uncomfortable but what followed was even more unexpected. After a cursory round of questions, the director of the program, Dr. Hakemi informed her that these students were coming from mixed backgrounds, from school drop-outs to college graduates, both from very conservative to slightly liberal ideology systems. In order for her to better understand how the setup worked, Dr. Hakemi explained to her the college designed this program to aid students learn English especially to those foreign students who would be working in India. In addition to teaching, she was to assist them in their general development and cultural adjustment along with the good use of English, taking into consideration that speaking in the target language was paramount. Just when Maya was feeling a little confident, Dr. Hakemi announced that she should be introduced to the students and be given a demonstration of the program module. The director sent for Mrs. Lalli Mohammed, the lead professor. After a brief introduction by Dr. Hakemi, Maya followed Mrs. Lalli to a classroom. Later, Maya found to her joy that Mrs. Lalli (short for Lolita) also came from Calcutta and was a Bengali married to an Iranian. The remaining vestige of nervousness disappeared and was replaced by elation. Mrs. Lalli then proceeded to teach a lesson in front of her. The demo also served as an introduction of her future students. The students were in their early to late twenties. They were inquiring about Maya; they were restless and somewhat immature. She wondered whether she was cut out for this job and could manage such students. She had no time to be pondering over this, she told herself, as she tried paying attention to Mrs. Lalli's lesson. One more visit to Dr. Hakemi's office and Maya was through with the interview.

The job was hers, he advised her.

She had plenty of time on her hands and did not want to go back to Priya's, so she looked for a telephone booth to call home and tell her parents of the recent development.

"Hello ma? It's Maya."

"Maya, why haven't you called? We were so worried."

"I was busy ma. Remember, I am still trying to adapt to my new city."

"Well, when are you coming back?"

"Ma, I am not going back there, at least not now."

"What? Why not? Don't you think that we're upset too with everything that happened? Everybody here keeps asking about you, I don't know what to say"

"Ma, how can you even mention these other people, where were they when we needed them? Have you forgotten when I was bedridden in the hospital crying for days with bottles of saline attached to my arm? Don't talk about them, please! Anyway, tell father that I called and give him my love. Please, tell him not to worry. I will try and call up again soon. Ok? You take care."

"Maya, I want you to come back, please. We are not happy with you over there, are you listening?" asked her mother, almost crying.

"I love you ma, but I need time, ok? I will call you later, bye" said Maya, as she hung up the phone. She felt miserable for speaking in such way to her mother when she didn't mean to. She had to be strong so she wouldn't get swayed by her mother. Maya wasn't feeling as excited as she had been earlier. The dreadful past from which she was running from seemed determined to cling to her. She knew that finding sympathy from her family was too much to ask of them. That's why she avoided bringing up that subject.

That night at home, she gave Priya the details of her interview, the demo class and her future students. She also confessed the misconception she had about Iranians. She thought they dressed in long, full covered dresses and women in Burka (a loose garment covering the entire body and having a veiled opening for the eyes). Instead, women covered their head with a scarf and wore a dress called Monto, which had been shortened considerably in modern times: a far cry from the traditional Burka. She told her how instead of an army of solemn Burqua clad women she found a flock of very attractive and beautiful women: most of them had big almond-shaped eyes with long eyelashes, and they were either brunettes or blondes. Maya found out later that a lot of people in the northern part of Iran had blonde hair and light-colored eyes. She also found out that beautiful features were accentuated with beautiful clothes. Maya noticed men and women equally gave immense importance to being well-dressed. The women paid attention to cosmetics and took notice to the ongoing fashion in America. It seemed to her that they lived as Americans in their mind no matter how far they were from it. Maya was equally surprised to learn how innocent they were even after surviving the ravages of war with Iraq for those long eight years. She could see something similar in their eyes to those of village children in India eons ago, when a simple hello and a smile made them burst into fits of laughter and where any friendly gesture was greatly appreciated. But alas! Those days are gone taking with them the small pleasures of life. Maya felt her eyes filled with tears. It was heartbreaking for her to see how times had changed indeed and there were no remains left. Maya was overwhelmed with a mental turmoil caused by the ups and downs she had gone through in the past months.

Priya told her that a salary of eight thousand was really measly in Bangalore, and pretty soon she would have to leap into something that would offer more money. "It's ok for now honey, even great for a novice, but teaching permanently? It's a little too staid!"

"No, it is fine for me, I like it" said Maya.

"But then, how can you be sure, you have never taught a soul before?" asked Priya. "Umm, yes, maybe true but I have a feeling about it that …"

"Well it's the first break so far, and it won't be the last. But remember, everything is so expensive here and you want your independence, which I think is a good thing, so how are you going to manage?" Asked Priya surprised.

Maya cringed inwardly at such bluntness and silently vowed to move out of there as soon as she had a chance. She knew this task would be hard but she would find a way. Borrowing money from her parents eventually had to stop. But at least she was learning to cope in difficult times and the lesson was not in vain. Who would have ever thought that bright good-looking Maya would end up like this? Abused and bruised mentally and physically. A failure even before she got a chance to start. Her heart still ached for her unborn baby. In any case, she was not giving up so easily and was proud of herself for taking the first step to bettering her life. Still there was a fragment of nagging doubt that she might not make it in the end as was put in time and again by Avik. "You are too lazy! You're always daydreaming! All the big lectures you give me, you should go out into the real world and check it out." Maya heard his insults in her head again. Maya wanted to erase these vicious words out of her head; they were like knife cuts. She felt worthless and like a complete loser. "The only thing you are good at is cooking" Avik told her once. Maya refused to find answers to Avik's unloving ways. She had been through enough. She was not going to make excuses of what should have been. Today was a day to relax and celebrate. But she was not sure about the celebration part because they neither have plans for the evening nor plans to meet the entire gang. Strangely enough she wanted it to happen so she could meet at Aakash's place as they had previously planned. Maya laughed at the thought of her heart titillating for a man she barely knew.

The next day, Priya had had a meeting with her boss to go over the last assignment she successfully concluded. She was elated because she was sure that her performance would not go unnoticed and reflect positively on her KPA (Key Performance Area) for a salary raise. She had been waiting for this opportunity for a long time. This meant she could rent the flat she had seen with Dhiraj at Cox Town. It was located right on a main road where she would have accessibility to rickshaws in the morning. It was a charming two-bedroom apartment with a small kitchen and a balcony overlooking the playground of the building next door. They were already planning how they were going to turn this small flat into a cute and cozy den of love. Dhiraj was really keen on the idea of moving in together. His business had kept him away from home time and again. He was the second son and he had done well for himself. His older brother on the other hand, was closer to their father. Although they loved Dhiraj, he was sometimes considered the prodigal son. So when Priya mentioned this flat he was ecstatic and wanted to see it. He wanted to give a security deposit right away but Priya being more cautious asked him to wait until she got her salary raise. She wanted to contribute with the rent since they were a couple now. After talking it over Dhiraj convinced Priya to at least put down a deposit. He asked her to go by herself since he had a business trip scheduled for Singapore. Thinking she could do that the next day, Priya decided to take her lunch break before meeting her client when the intercom buzzed. "Yes?" Priya answered.

"Priya, it's Rita. Listen, how about going to our usual joint after work? Girls only!" "Today?" asked Priya.

"Yeah, it's Wednesday, Ladies Night! And I need to unwind." "What? Don't tell me, some new kid on the block?"

"Yes sweetie" almost purred Rita.

"Hmmm, actually I was planning to do something with Maya, spend some time with her … she got this new job as a teacher …."

"Fine no problem! Why don't both of you join me around 8:00 p.m. then?"

"You know her! But wait, I'll just tell her you have some good news to share"

"Great! It's settled then, at 8:00, bye."

"Bye" said Priya and sat holding the receiver thinking whether to call Maya now or later. She thought it would be best to call her later so she wouldn't have time to make any excuses.

Aakash had just finished lunch and decided to take a stroll along Brigade Road. Having an office close to the heart of Bangalore had certain advantages. For one, it offered a kaleidoscope of human activity that kept one engrossed. Secondly, one could always take a stroll and rekindle one's creativity if it was lost. But this was never a problem with Aakash; the art of photography was indeed a gift as far as he was concerned. It was this hobby that made him popular in college and the girls followed, of course. An attractive young man with a talent so promising it would make a difference in his time. His professors always said he had a bright future ahead of him. He came from a wealthy family hence attracting a lot of girls and their greedy mothers. But to their disappointment, girls were not what made him get up in the morning. It was his acute interest in photography that kept him going. He took his classes and his photography seriously unlike other young men his age who decorated the walls of their rooms with pin-ups of Pamela Anderson and posters of the Indian demy goddess Aishwariya Rai.[4]

Aakash's room on the other hand, was devoid of any adornments. His bed was most of the time strewn with big fat books of Raghu Rai, Satyajit Ray's on photography, and books on advertisement. His hobby was seen and felt all around him after his father gave him a Nikon camera with professional zoom lens as a gift. His mother saw this as a fad and an expensive hobby but nothing more. She always thought her son had the potential to achieve greatness. He would be the topic of conversation in her innumerable high-society parties but it turned out later, to her horror, a serious career move for her son. Had he gone mad? It was inconceivable for the Poorie family their beta or son, Puneet Poorie had become impossible to talk to. For a typical Punjabi family belonging to the high society of Delhi, this was a catastrophe unparallel in their entire Bieradree (community). Sons are meant to follow their father's footsteps and join the family business. Another upheaval the Poorie family experienced was when their son adamantly pursued a girl he met at a bus stop. To

[4]An award-winning South Indian actress who won the Miss World title in 1994.

make matters worse, she was from a different community. It was obvious to Mrs. Poorie this girl had no money. Her son's courtship of this mysterious girl and everything surrounding her became an everlasting enigma. As reserved as Puneet was, he didn't give his mother the pleasure of getting a word out of him nor giving up his girl. He finished college and his romance with the mysterious girl grew stronger to the consternation of his entire family. As days went by, the rift and the tension among the family increased. The situation got out of control one day; without warning Puneet left the family for good under the pretext of going to the university and never came back.

The family never heard from him and he never looked for them. Only Anil, his friend in Bangalore knew the real story. Puneet told him he was speeding as he eloped with his beloved girlfriend, Sheila. He wanted to start a new life even if it meant without his parents' blessing. Unfortunately, their car was hit by a speeding truck trying to evade the police. They lay in their shattered car on a highway under the darkness of night. Daylight brought the harsh reality that he survived and his girlfriend had perished. She was found lifeless, mangled under all the metal. That was the end of Puneet as everybody knew him. This tragedy brought a change in him. He felt he was given a second chance at life so he decided to capture every moment of life through his lens. Ten days after he was released from the hospital he started his new life as Aakash Poorie and headed to his friend's house in Bangalore. "Puneet Poorie is dead" Aakash said somberly to himself. His life took off almost immediately as he became one of the directors in the advertisement agency he started with Anil, his friend in Bangalore. His avid interest in photography turned into a fine art for making documentaries. He used this to his advantage and put it to work; in as little as five years he had established a reputable business. His new firm, Inspiration Unlimited started giving his competitors a run for their money.

Since he had finished all his pending work for the day, Aakash decided to take it easy in the afternoon. Before the traffic light turned green, he lit a cigarette and stood scanning the people on the street through the cloud of white smoke that he exhaled. Suddenly, he noticed a woman wearing a blue dress on the opposite street. She looked familiar. "I think I know her" he said to himself "Yes! It's Maya" he exclaimed. Strangely, he almost felt excited and found himself smiling. He hadn't felt this eager towards women since the death of his girlfriend. He wanted to draw attention to her, to have her acknowledge his presence but she stared ahead of her in a pensive way. He hesitated whether to call out her name or not. Before he got the courage to do it, she disappeared before his eyes. An intrusive and insignificant rickshaw came and whisked her away. "Damn" he cursed out loud. He really wanted to meet her again. Ever since he met her at The Taste of China something had happened to him. He felt different. For reasons unknown to him, Maya inspired a caring feeling in him. Could this be love? Could he love again? Could Maya fill the emptiness in his heart? He didn't want to believe that another woman could take Sheila's place. No, he shook his head -this couldn't be love. He believed that true love only happened once in a lifetime. This was one thing he truly believed and preached with equal valor. He didn't consider himself a romantic fool and thought love was overrated. Aakash knew he was fooling himself and couldn't deny he felt something in his heart. An overwhelming feeling of sadness and loneliness embraced him.

Checking his wristwatch he decided to head back to the office to keep his mind occupied and off his past. It was easier to deal with work, which he considered comforting at times than to deal with his thoughts, which he couldn't control. But destiny had other things in store for him. As soon as he reached the office, an absolute pandemonium met him. For starters the fax machine was not working; all the phones were ringing as they were not going through the switchboard but straight to the direct lines because of a fault in the EPBX. There were few lit candles on the table, meaning the electricity had just been restored. As soon as the receptionist-cum-administrator saw Aakash, she approached him immediately. Sarita, normally a poised girl, was agitated and stressed today.

"Thank God you are here Sir."

"Where is the fire Sarita?" asked Aakash dryly.

"Now there's no fire, but I received a call from the Nat Geos, Mumbai office, and there was no one to handle it, and they said it was very, very important." Sarita said exasperated.

"Why? What's wrong? Why didn't you put Anil on line?" Asked Aakash irritated. "That's because, number one; he's not here, and number two; they only wanted to speak to you. So that's that!" said Sarita with a worried look on her face. Aakash patted her on the shoulder as a reconciliatory gesture and went to his desk to return the urgent call he's been informed of. Nonetheless, he was annoyed by Anil's uncharacteristic behavior of leaving the office unannounced. When they started the business together, they agreed to never leave the office unattended; either he or Anil would always be present in the office. This business venture was their passion and as directors they couldn't afford to make a mistake. From small advertisements to creating jingles, over the last five years, they have moved onto making documentaries and corporate advertisement. They made four documentaries for the Forest Department of India, two for the Tourism Department, and two that started as a labor of love filming the hill people, which later got acclaimed by The National Geographic channel and wanted to use it for their Nat Geo section. So it was no longer a hobby, but serious business. As Aakash dialed the number, a feeling of satisfaction invaded his entire body knowing the work he submitted was approved. A pleasant surprise was still awaiting; the channel wanted a sequel to the last documentary, which they were planning to broadcast within the next two months. Time was of essence and he needed to carry out this project at once. His restored confidence instantly replaced the scene in his head where he found himself speechless in front of Maya. He was reminiscing on his botched encounter earlier when the phone rang. It was Gaurav inviting to join him for a drink after work. Gaurav insisted and didn't take no for an answer. He gave him a guilt trip and reminded he needed a break. So they agreed to meet at Soirée, a restaurant on Church Road.

Maya stepped into the shower and as she lathered she kept repeating to herself "Yes, yes, I did it!" She had gotten a job on her own. She was capable of achieving goals. Her confidence and talents had always been crushed by Avik. What would he have said now? She felt no qualm in stirring up the ghost of the past. She began to relax as the water coursed over her body washing away doubts and her bitter past. She was refreshed and in a happy mood, too restless for her own comfort. Surprisingly, she didn't want to stay home tonight hiding herself from the world. Unfortunately, she didn't know what to do or where to go. She didn't expect Priya home before 9:00 p.m. as it was her usual schedule. On any given day Maya would have been satisfied either reading or watching TV. Not tonight though. She was feeling a little lonely and unsettled. While she was stirring the tea she prepared, the phone rang.

"Hello?" she answered.

"Hi, what are you doing up?" asked Priya.

"Hi Priya, today I am too excited to do my normal stuff."

"Well, well, that's a good start! I must say the new job has had a good influence on you" said Priya.

"How come you're calling at this time?"

"Well, that's because I think today you ought to celebrate. It's a real step towards your future, a real bold step!"

"Celebrate, how? It's a weekday and you are still working!" said Maya hesitantly. She just could not believe her ears, for it was exactly what she wanted to do.

"That's not a problem. In fact, Rita will also join us and we can all go to our usual joint, Soirée. It's a fabulous lounge-restaurant. We can have dinner there."

"That sounds good! So, when do we meet?"

"Be ready by 7:30, we will pick you up, ok?"

"Yes!" Maya said happily.

"… and please wear something different and more suited for the occasion, in one word something interesting. Done?" Priya said firmly.

"Well, I am not sure if I have anything like that, most of my clothing is Indian outfits." Maya said uncertainly. "Wear the black trousers you bought the other day. You can borrow one of my tops to go with it. And don't forget the rest, I mean your make-up and all that." "Aye, aye Sir" said Maya meekly.

"Good then, we meet at 7:30. Bye" Said Priya and hung up.

Soirée was a cool joint, very contemporary as far as décor, look and ambiance were concerned. Men and women in clusters were walking, chatting, laughing and lending an atmosphere of pure fun and excitement, an evening full of promise. The majority of the patrons were dressed in black in a wide variety of modern outfits: short sleeves, long skirts, minis, micros, halter and backless wonders. Tube and tank tops seemed to be wading in and out of the place. She noticed a lot of young adults stepping out of cars, queuing up on the staircase while having their hand stamped to show their rightful presence in there. Maya was relieved that she listened to her friend today and tried something new in keeping with the ongoing fashion parade in black. She wore a pair of black pants and a black and red diagonal pattern sleeveless top. The deep V exposed her cleavage, making her uneasy and unable to relax completely. This was totally different from her style. Maya always prided in on her elegance and overall demeanor through her clothes. So today's attire including the place was totally incongruous. Chewing on her trepidation, she joined the others on the elevator and reached the second floor of the restaurant.

The zen-inspired décor created with strategic lighting, water flowing in canals on both sides of the corridor, and the sweet lotus smell pervaded the scene. Maya looked around in joy and deeply inhaled the air all around. She noticed as they continued walking further down that the place was divided into sections. As planned they headed towards the bar. Even though, this was not her first time at a bar she felt differently about the whole experience. This time she was determined to enjoy it. The bar had its usual trappings and after settling themselves comfortably they ordered their drinks. Maya ordered a Piña Colada. She thought if would be safer than whisky or beer. They chose the sofa at the extreme corner and sat down excitedly to share their respective tales.

"So, what's this new job of yours Maya?" asked Rita.

"Well, it's a job as an English teacher for foreign students."

"That should be interesting. I take it is not a conventional set up?" asked Rita.

"Let me explain" Priya interrupted. It's a step-in for Iranian students who have to learn English to pursue a higher education here in India. Maya is to make it happen for them."

"Wow! That's really cool! It sounds very promising. I am saying this because there are good looking dudes in this community." Rita said grinning broadly.

"Come on, Rita, you are getting far too excited and missing the important point …" Maya said.

"And that is?" Rita grumbled impatiently.

"They will be at least ten years my junior if not more" concluded Maya.

"But of course, how stupid of me" said Rita sarcastically.

"But enough about me, why don't you tell us your news? Priya told me something interesting is brewing" said Maya.

"Well, I am not sure, maybe, maybe not?"

"Now what is that supposed to mean?" asked Priya exasperated "Is there a guy or not?"

"Naturally, what I meant is I am not sure if I am reading too much into it as usual, or there is really something."

"First, tell me how long this has been going on?" asked Priya.

"Well … I guess about two months."

"Two months? Then it started after we met, that's nice," said Maya.

"Only two months!" Priya exclaimed. "Do I know him; I hope it's not anyone you met in a party?"

"Yes, you do know him, and no, I did not meet him in a party. Really, what do you take me for?"

"Well, if you want me to keep guessing then you got to give me more details. Where does he work?"

"He works in a bank."

"In a Bank? Well, who is he? I can't remember such guy, so just tell us, ok? No more suspense, and let us order some more snacks and drinks." After a brief gap that was taken up mostly in ordering another round of drinks and more food, they all settled down and resumed their conversation. Seeing Priya getting so worked up in not a desirable way Rita decided to come out with the name without any more ado. "It's Gaurav."

"You mean all this suspense for him?" Asked Priya.

"Well, what about it? Are you not interested anymore?" Rita asked a little sullenly. "Of course we are! Just that we couldn't imagine it was him" said Maya trying to placate Rita.

"So, what do you think Priya? Is it going to be any different this time? It better be!" said Rita and grabbed her third glass of gin and tonic.

"Hey not so fast, take it easy," said Priya and gently but firmly took her glass away. "Maybe it will work out this time. As I always say, it is never too late for the right thing to happen, and optimism always pays. But just to be on the safe side, why not do some more homework on him?"

"What kind of homework?" Rita asked.

"Like finding out his whereabouts" said Priya.

"You mean snooping? That really sucks, I can't get that low, not for a man" said Rita with finality.

"I kind of agree with Priya on this. It's better to be safe than sorry. We can ask his friends or someone working at the same bank." said Maya in a conciliatory tone.

"Yes exactly! Which bank?" Priya said enthusiastically.

"People's Bank" Rita simply said.

"Hmmm, maybe I can help. I know someone who will not mind doing me a favor." said Priya.

"That's great! So Rita, stop worrying now and let's enjoy the evening. I am feeling happy myself thanks to you and Priya, and I want to continue feeling like this as long as possible. The beer also does not taste half as bad as I thought it would. At least it tastes far better than the syrup that I have been drinking" said Maya laughing.

"Yeah! Why not hit the floor and do some Tango?" said Rita almost jumping up from the sofa.

"Yes, sure, three to Tango" said Priya and followed suit, pulling along the half-confused and somewhat undecided Maya. Shortly afterwards, Maya started getting more comfortable with the ambiance of the place. Her concoction of Piña Coladas and a couple of beers were making her increasingly happy and carefree.

The music became an incoherent jumble of notes and chords with loud heart-pounding beats. The air, heavy with smoke, along with the interplay of lights and shades transformed the place into a land of mystery where the dark silhouettes kept moving around. Some people stood watching while others danced, and the warm musky odor of expensive perfumes mixed with sweat, engulfed Maya completely. The bright spotlights along with the dancing lights were making it difficult for Maya to keep herself steady on the floor. The loud music put the dancers in a trance in a state of ecstasy almost. They were pushing and shoving, dancing with gay abandon. The drinks along with these other stimuli were making her queasy and slightly giddy. Priya and Rita were out of sight. She no longer knew who she was dancing with. She vaguely remembered that someone snatched her original partner a while back. Her current partner, a pudgy pushy guy was turning her evening into a nightmare and she was desperately trying to escape from him. He continuously pulled her closer to the point she could smell his whisky breath. She was on the verge of tears when she felt someone gripped her arm strongly and pulled her sideways off the dance floor. She found herself in the arms of a man who was guiding her to a sofa. As soon as she caught her breath she tried to turn her face to see who had rescued her from that Neanderthal. The man came close to her face and whispered

"Have you had enough fun or did I interrupt something" Lo and behold! Maya couldn't believe her eyes. It was Aakash.

"What are you doing here?" Maya said surprised.

"No, I think I should be asking that question" Aakash said in a dry tone.

"No you got it all wrong" said Maya in a feeble voice.

"No, I think the rest of the people here would agree with me to what

I just witnessed. For a moment I thought you were dancing with your Siamese twin." Aakash said sarcastically.

"Believe me, he was pulling me and wouldn't let go of me …" she paused and lowered her voice to say "I don't even know who he is."

"What? I just don't get it. You don't know that guy and both of you were on each other's arms?" asked Aakash incredulously. It was exactly at this moment that her annoying dancing partner showed up looking for her. Before she even had a chance to explain the situation to Aakash, the guy headed straight towards Maya with the intention of taking her back to the dance floor. Looking at the expression on Maya's face, Aakash turned and spotted him. In a jiffy, he stood up and faced the guy ready to clobber him. Maya looked desperately for any signs of Priya or Rita but there was none. Maya never liked confrontations. She avoided them at all cost and to her dismay she was about to witness one. She prayed it wouldn't escalate to a fight. She wanted to make herself invisible as she feared the outcome. Maya became paralyzed and couldn't utter a word. She wanted to convey her thoughts and tell the guys she wouldn't become an spectator to the pair showing off.

She, the woman, had no role whatsoever. Wasn't it always this way: Women, the mute spectators? Really, thought Maya, these days she was turning into a thinker, albeit little morbid. Sudden situations, that at odd times were making her think and feel the way she had never done before. Tears of bitterness sprang into her eyes. The word mute spectator really hurt her; as she realized that one has greater power to hurt oneself than others can possibly do. Others come to our lives at different times and in different situations and their ability to heal or hurt us, rests solely on our own power to let them or stop them.

Look at myself, thought Maya, how I go ahead to hurt myself some more by calling myself a mute spectator? How many women before me had done that knowingly, and unknowingly? Sometimes they defy their state; sometimes they comply, but accepting centuries of injustice and oppressions. At times smiling, and sometimes screaming for help, but watching all the same. Rows and rows of women standing and watching their lives being dictated and lived by preferences not their own, of choices not made by them, of conditions not laid by them, of being mute spectators of their abuse –spiritual, emotional, physical- of their whole essence.

Maya knew in her heart she could make decisions, be strong and determined. However, in this situation she could only watch and accept the circumstances she was in. The guy may have been drunk enough to grope a woman on the dance floor but was sane enough to identify danger when he faced one, and he did spot it in Aakash. So he stopped hastily and throwing both his hands in the air in the final gesture of surrender said "Sorry man didn't know she was busy." Promptly he did the vanishing act and was gone before Aakash had a chance to show him the way back. Finally Priya showed up and caught the frantic wave of Maya calling her. She joined them and soon Gaurav followed. Once all gathered sitting on the sofa, the rest of them who were more laid back agreed it had all been a big misunderstanding. Hence, they decided to leave the place. Since Maya was very tired, embarrassed, and angry at the whole situation she gladly welcomed the suggestion. Aakash took charge immediately and decided to call it a day and drop the girls at home. It was past midnight and Maya not being used to such outings was about to say yes, when all hell broke loose.

"Hey man, what got into you? What are you talking about? We just got here!" said Gaurav in disbelief.

"Really, Aakash don't be such a grouch and pack us home!" whined Rita.

"Well then count me out! I am in no mood to go club hopping. I can do without a replay of what I saw" concluded Aakash looking at Maya. Priya felt Maya's uneasiness and sensed something was amiss with her friend. She decided to confront Aakash about it.

"What replay are you talking about Aakash?"

"We can discuss that later Priya, let's go now. I've had enough of this place." Maya piped in quickly.

"We can do that, or we can do something different" suggested Priya.

"Like what?" asked Gaurav.

"We could buy some food and booze, and go over to my place, how about that?"

"Hey that's great, we can chill without being annoyed." Rita said giving an insinuating look at Gaurav.

"Ok, we could certainly do that" said Gaurav turning to Aakash "Is this fine with you?"

"Yes, I think this is something we can all do" said Aakash.

"Good then, let's hop into my car and hit your pad. What say you hon?" said Gaurav pulling Rita closer to him.

"Mmm … I say great!" purred Rita.

It was just past 1:00 a.m. when they arrived at Priya's doorstep. Another ten minutes to realize that Priya's keys had gone missing sometime during the evening and they were locked out. Neither the situation at hand nor time seemed to be of any inconvenience to the newly-found couple; it became a sore spot for the rest. While Priya kept turning out the contents of her immaculate bag imagining the keys to appear at each attempt, Maya was desperately trying not to tumble due to her inebriated state. With Aakash towering so close, she did not want to give the impression that she was incapable of taking care of herself. To make matters worse, her bladder was full to its peak due to all the drinks she consumed at the restaurant. All she could do now was to stand with her legs drawn together to avoid an accident. Seeing herself in this situation, Maya reminisced when she was seven years old and she played dark room religiously. In those high-tension moments hiding, keeping perfectly still in a small dark room crowded with the rest of her playmates, she resorted to this method of crossing her legs since a toilet break was not allowed. Maya wondered whether she was strange to think of such matters at a time like this or did the child in her always sneaked out at odd moments? Finding Priya's keys had been a fiasco so they decided to move the gathering to Aakash's flat instead. Nobody complained at the fact they were driving like hooligans at break-neck speed. They covered the entire distance from MG Road to JP Nagar Phase-I in twenty minutes when it normally took about forty minutes.

En route, they stopped to pick up drinks and food. Everyone was relieved to have finally arrived, especially Maya who rushed straight to the toilet. They made themselves comfortable in the small cozy one-bedroom flat. Priya headed for the kitchen with the food and drinks to assist Aakash. The lovebirds went straight to the entertaining center and were looking through the collection of CDs Askash had. They were giggling and whispering to each other. As Maya came out of the bathroom, she saw how romantically close Rita and Gaurav were dancing locked into each other's arms, lost to the famous ballad "The Power of Love" co-written and originally recorded by Jennifer Rush. Maya smiled as she thought it was a sweet tender sight; love budding before her eyes. Her smile vanished though when she locked eyes with Aakash, who was standing near the CD player with a drink in his hand. Mockery gleamed in his eyes and he finally said to Maya "What a pity we had to leave your Siamese twin behind!" Fuming Maya turned away, refusing to take the bait. Aakash obviously did not want to let her go and said "If I had known you would sulk due to his absence, I would have invited him to join us instead of chasing him away."

"What are you suggesting Mr. Poorie?" asked Maya in a cold tone.

"I'm not suggesting, but saying it" said in an arrogant tone. Standing straight with her arms crossed Maya tried to defend herself saying "I find your insinuation highly offensive."

"Well, I for one found the whole scene offensive and cheap."

"How dare you?" said Maya while raising herself on her toes to slap him. However, fatigue plus the high level of alcohol in her system got the best of Maya. Thus, instead of slapping him she lost balance and fell forward. Aakash broke her fall, grabbed her raised hand and twisted in a way she found herself in his arms. Holding her tightly, he purred in her ear "Now what are you going to do? Who's going to rescue you now?" "Leave me alone, just let me go!" struggled Maya.

"I should teach you a lesson instead" he said menacingly.

"No! Don't you dare!"

"Dare Maya?" asked Aakash and exerted some more pressure on her arm.

"Ok, I'm sorry! Please, stop hurting me, just let me go!" She sobbed.

"Well, that's better; the softer side of a woman is what I like in a lady." Maya was reduced to tears; she felt humiliated and helpless from the whole incident. At that moment Priya appeared and enthusiastically announced she had found her keys. "Hey guys, I finally found my keys, they had slipped within the lining of the wretched bag, I can relax now and enjoy the rest of the evening." Her announcement was received with a lukewarm response of a simple "Oh that's great" from Gaurav. Priya looked at the corner and saw two pairs of lips busy exploring each other not leaving much room for replying. Aakash in the meantime straighten himself and let go of Maya.

"So how about a small drink for me Aakash? A nightcap perhaps" Priya asked.

"Sure, what is it, whiskey?"

"Yeah, and let's eat! We haven't had anything to eat since early this evening. What about you Maya?"

"I am going to make her a glass of fresh lime and prepare her a nice meal" interjected Aakash before Maya could utter a word.

"Good, what about you guys? Rita?" asked Priya raising her eyebrow as she didn't like how desperately she looked kissing Gaurav. Fearful of where this might lead her friend to, she insisted they should eat something. That would definitely put an end to all that kissing, she reasoned.

"Oh, we are just fine, but could do with a drink" the reply came from Gaurav.

"For goodness sake! You can make your drink, and Rita, I suggest that you have some food!" Said Priya ferociously.

"Ok relax, I will make my drink" said Gaurav.

Maya decided to seek shelter in the bathroom. She could not face the probing eyes of her friend nor could she come up with a verbatim narration of what had transpired between herself and Aakash. Splashing cold water on her face made her feel better. However, looking at her reflection on the big, black-rimmed mirror Maya noticed her eye make-up was washed away. The remnants were all smudged giving a haunted look to her eyes. She stared at the mirror for a while and mused how her initial fun at Soirée followed by the mishap on the dance floor and later compounded by Aakash's unexpected arrival, turned the evening into a high tension drama. She could not believe how such a propitious evening, full of energy and fun turned out to be a disaster. Were all the important things meant to end suddenly? She gazed down her chest to look for her Lord Ganesh pendant and holding it tightly she asked him to explain why she was the chosen one to be deprived of a normal life. Why did her marriage have to dwindle away to bitterness? Why did such a small pleasure, like this evening, turn out this way? She knew her god would not reply and she had to find the answers herself. She figured maybe some day when time had seasoned her amply the answers would be there. The bitterness of the past would be wiped out and she would learn to be comfortable around men once again. As if in response to the line of her thought, the little scene with Aakash came to mind. Unknowingly she touched the places where he had touched her. She caressed the cheek where his face had brushed while he purred menacingly into her ear. The memory of his warm breath on her neck and ears gave her goose bumps. She felt ashamed for reliving those moments and feeling this way. Hurriedly she tidied her face, put a little lipstick on and quickly braided her hair with a rubber band she found lying between the bottles of after-shave and mouthwash in the medicine cabinet. Satisfied to seeing more of the old Maya reflected on the mirror she snapped shut the cabinet and stepped out.

She was stung by hunger looking at the way both Priya and Rita were engrossed in their food. The aroma wafting to her nose was too much to resist. She did not mind spending some more time at Aakash's place as long as she ate. She did not even mind the way Gaurav was picking the food off Rita's plate. Normally it would have disgusted her but now hunger superseded everything. Keeping a dispassionate ear to the ongoing conversation, she kept wondering where he could have vanished in the last half hour. Shortly after he walked in and said: "Well, I have garaged the car and locked the gate." Surprised, Maya asked "Why, are we not going home Priya?" "No, we will spend whatever is left of the night here and go in the morning. Rita has the day off tomorrow and I will go late. Besides, Aakash doesn't mind if we stay here."

"I can call in sick tomorrow and baby-sit you, girls" said Gaurav almost toppling over trying to steal a kiss from Rita. Gaurav is becoming a nuisance, thought Priya giving him a dirty look. As if sensing it Aakash said "That is okay, but I suggest we call it a day now. Both me and Gaurav will make ourselves comfortable here, while you girls help yourselves in my bedroom." Taking the cue from him, both Priya and Maya headed toward the bedroom. Rita needed a further prod so Gaurav helped her up.

Maya felt tired to the bone, and was glad to be in bed and under covers. She sought to delay the onset of sleep to mull over the recent events. She closed her eyes and feigned sleep; she could not help thinking and admiring how easily Aakash had taken things under control, said the appropriate words and handled the situation with authority. Contrary to Avik who never took charge in any matter, instead she took the reins as if she were the man of the house. Her growing years were taken up by keeping a watchful eye over Nikhil and over her own natural curiosity towards men. This was intensified by the many stories of love escapades that she had heard form her friends, mostly Beaz. The speed with which she took to men and discarded them alarmed Maya. Still the male species continued to enchant and interest her and she became all too willing to throw all caution to wind when she met Avik for the first time. In her drowsy state, Maya went on reminiscing how she was introduced to Avik at Beaz's birthday party. They hit it off almost immediately. They started seeing each other and after a couple of dates later they had professed undying love. Even though he never uttered the "M" (marriage) word Maya took that as the only natural outcome of their soaring hormonal state. After many protests and heated arguments with his parents, who wanted at all cost to prevent marriage from taking place due to socio-economic disparity; Maya convinced Avik to stand up for their love. It also prompted her to convince her parents of the same. However, Nikhil was not too sure of Avik's lasting love for his sister. He told her straight off that he found Avik, a tad too effeminate – a man with weak personality, hence not a match for his sister. Before drifting off to sleep, Maya mused that Nikhil was more mature than she had ever given him credit for. The "tad" he had warned her about turned out to be a "load" over the years and Nikhil already the apple of their parents' eye naturally swung all support in his favor. How she had hated him then for proving himself to be right. Destiny proved him to be a better judge of character.

And now Aakash … but even before she could finish mulling over his name, sleep finally overpowered her and when she opened her eyes again it was morning. Focusing her eyes on the heavily curtained room for a moment made her realize she was not at home. She was coming to terms with the course of events that had landed her in this room. Nonetheless, she was surprised to find herself alone. Was it not a day off for Rita? What about Priya? She said she would go in late. Then, what about Aakash? Where is he? Maya wondered. The house was silent. She checked her watch and she was surprised to see it was already noon. She jumped up from the bed at once and got ready. On her way out, she found two notes addressed to her on the music system next to a key. The first one gave her instructions regarding the key and the second one began...

You looked so vulnerable and innocent as you slept, I wanted to take you in my arms; I think that underneath that surface there's a child hiding. Oh, by the way, next time you go out, I suggest you have milk instead. Alcohol doesn't agree with you. Remember that for when we meet in the future, which I pray for it to be soon.

Yours truly,

Aakash

It took a lot of self-control on her part not to break anything as she stormed out of his place.

Maya's tryst with the Iranian community began the day of her job interview, which lasted two hours plus the demo class and introduction to her students. She was thrilled to get a real job and a steady salary as well. Doing odd jobs here and there and modeling on occasion had not given her a chance to save a lot of money. This job was her savior; she would learn how to manage her finances and time, thus becoming independent at last. Her mood level elevated as she thought this. Moreover, she was delighted with the idea of being in a setting where she would be exposed to a new culture. She realized then, she would not only be teaching English to these Iranian students but she would be learning from them as well. Eager, yet anxious Maya stepped out the elevator on the seventh floor of the Global English Center. She was finally writing a new chapter in her life, Maya thought as she signed the register and waited for Dr. Hakemi.

Maya realized she had to get acquainted with her new environment gradually; something she had done in the past. A few minutes later Dr. Hakemi appeared and greeted Maya. He went over some class procedures and policy. He handed her some books and school material as he emphasized on two main issues: she had to teach in the target language and had to be strict with the students since she was substituting for a teacher who had taken a leave of absence. As he did this, he welcomed her aboard and wished her luck. She felt an overwhelming affliction creeping up from her toes to her head. The onus was on her to gain the students' confidence and manage until their regular teacher returned. She definitely would have preferred to teach a brand new group for she knew how students take advantage of the situation; whereas this group was already accustomed to the teacher that started the cycle. To cross that bridge posed a challenge in itself.

Maya entered the classroom, greeted the students and lay her materials on the desk. She looked at the roster and twirling the pen in her hands she studied their names: Ahmed, Maryam, Bejad, Bahare, Ajade, Alijani, Hamid, Erfan, Mohammad, Jaffar, Siavosh, Aida … she looked up and a cluster of inquisitive eyes stared back at her.

The silence in the class was overpowering, almost eerie. Maya scanned unsuccessfully among the aloof faces looking for a friendly smile. She breathed in and finally broke the silence by saying "I like to smile, what about you guys?" It worked! Almost in unison smiles drew on their faces. "I can see why" said a girl with big brown eyes wearing a bright scarf. "You have beautiful teeth" she added. The whole class burst out laughing. Maya had a big smile on her face and happiness started bubbling up inside her. This was a good sign indeed. She realized the students were looking for acceptance as much as she was. She knew this too well as she once looked for approval from her husband and his family.

She appreciated the bright-colored clothing of her students as it made her feel alive once again; it offered her a break from her colorless dreary past. She sighed with relief thinking this job was not going to be challenging after all. She breathed in her new environment and thanked Lord Ganesha, who certainly knew how to spruce up things in her life. Maya almost immediately recognized something special in this group of young adults and predicted the birth of a bond that would go beyond the confinement of the classroom. As the days passed by the rapport between Maya and the students grew and there was a sense of comradeship. In addition to her class modules, she discussed general subjects like the heartaches and disappointments they might encounter in life. She also discussed more serious topics such as the presence of 33 Crores[5] of Indian gods and goddesses and their myriad forms and incarnations, the saga of Indian culture rooting from the socio-economic, languages, religious diversity, customs, genetic background that has co-mingled over centuries. She tried to convey these complex topics in short

[5]A crore is a unit in the Indian numbering system, still widely used in Bangladesh, India, Maldives, Pakistan and Sri Lanka. An Indian crore is equal to 10 million (10^7).

uncomplicated phrases. From time to time she used a dose of theatrics which kept them engrossed. Amazingly, they all paid attention and demanded more. The students' quest for knowledge and desire to learn English also became one for Maya, as she rediscovered her own culture. Together they discovered the presence of French and German words in Persian along with Urdu, one of the 23 official languages of India. They found fascinating the fact that Sanskrit rooted in the cultures of South and Southeast Asia has evolved as well as influenced many modern-day languages of the world including Persian. Iranian men and women equally showed a passion for life something it was considered a myth shrouded on the literary pages of books or carefully woven political propaganda. It was their passion that stimulated the romance lying dormant in Maya. Maya recalled the trepidation of her first day of class and laughed about it. Now, she not only had won their confidence and their love but they started communicating better in English. It was rewarding for her as a teacher to see how much they had improved but it was equally gratifying for the students who had grown close to Maya. Their faces glowed with happiness when they discerned they could converse with their teacher. They became Maya's source of inspiration and the reason to wake up yet another day.

To show their appreciation for everything she had taught them, the students decided to invite Maya for lunch to their weekly gathering on Sunday. She was going to witness first-hand what their culture was all about. Now it was her turn to learn from them. She wore a white cotton long skirt flared at the bottom that complemented an empire-waist long sleeve top with a ruching effect; she matched it with a pair of delicately hand-painted porcelain earrings. The result was a younger looking Maya. She didn't look like a teacher but like a college student in love prancing to her destination. She hailed an auto and got in. For a split second, she wished Avik could see her, in this new found freedom as a competent and a contributing member of society. During her marriage, she had never been able to give the befitting replies to his criticisms, derogatory remarks and frequent jibes. She remained silent instead, sometimes with tear-brimming eyes and rarely refuted his accusations. She never understood how Avik could be so cruel towards another human being. She thought love conquered it all but she was wrong and she found out a little too late. Her idea of love was distorted living next to Avik.

Love to her was an all-encompassing emotion that took in its stride not only the positive qualities of a partner, but also the negative ones. She believed love was a profound passionate affection for another person with the ability to mold itself accordingly. Love could be found everywhere as long as she was next to her lover. While being married to Avik, this definition soon turned sour for Maya and swore it was overrated and misused. According to her new definition of love, this was just an evil conspiracy by society, a general misconception. She rationalized that the word "love" had been inflated to a degree for consumerism purposes: *I love my SUV, I love my cat, I love this dress, I love my cell phone, I love beer, etc.* Love in its purest form had been diminished from a feeling to an insignificant noun. As she sat in the auto en route to her destination, she wondered if there had ever been love between her and Avik. Nevertheless, she was learning and coming to terms with her new life as a divorcee. Her line of thought would have continued further had the auto driver not stopped and waited for her to get out. Already busy, looking for his next passenger, he informed her that Lingarajapuram was reached. He took his fare and left her standing on the sidewalk looking up at the building. Climbing to the second floor she had a panic attack and thought the whole thing to be quite absurd, possibly a bit too bold and surely out of line. She was not sure anymore if it was prudent for her to come to their house. What about the decorum of the teacher-student relationship? She certainly didn't want to break any rules or much less lose her job. She suddenly felt anxious; she couldn't picture herself starting all over again after having accomplished so much in the past few months. "Am I unconsciously sabotaging myself?" She said in a shaky voice. She didn't want to believe she could be responsible for jeopardizing her own career. Fully convinced of the absurdity of the situation, she was making her way back down the steps when one of her students spotted her from the balcony above and in glee shouted her name and announced her arrival to the rest. Her last effort at doing a vanishing act had to be aborted, as she retraced the steps once more and into their lives.

On the other side of town, Aakash was almost finished packing. The greater part of his luggage comprised the filming equipment. In addition, he had a huge camera bag filled with: a professional film SLR camera, a digital SLR camera, a 600mm Super-Telephotos lens, an AF-S 24-70mm f/2.8G ED lens, a video-camera, flash products, CDs, films, and memory cards. He put in two days change of undergarments and four Tee shirts. The pair of jeans he had on would be enough. The only thing left was the toiletries from the bathroom, which he started packing in a smaller tote bag as he waited for his colleague Anil to join him. The sequel to the tea growers was taking Anil and Aakash to the hills where they were going to spend the next four days interviewing these workers and filming the entire process of tea farming. It was this signature style of his —of living among the featured people, experiencing their daily lives first hand— what gave his work the winning edge. The modus-operandi of his systematic enquiry in the heart of the matter received accolades and helped in the selection process of the committee of the National Geographic. It was the success of the first part documentary about the flourishing tea industry in India, which convinced National Geographic that a sequel would be most suitable. They asked Aakash to select any tea farming state and make a documentary highlighting the tea production of that region in detail. As the avid traveler that he was, he always took advantage of this opportunity to use his camera to the fullest, in capturing memorable moments, unique snapshots of nature at its best, spontaneous frames of human faces. However, in one of his many trips he missed the hills of Uttaranchal, a beautiful and enchanting region of northern India and Himachal Pradesh, which has many undiscovered spots with unspoiled charm amidst nature. Fortunately for him, destiny would give him the opportunity again to see these amazing hills thanks to his line of work, which he combined with his passion for nature photography.

Aakash was eager to start this project and was immersed in his thoughts as he continued packing. He went to the bathroom to get his toiletries and as he opened his medicine cabinet something fell onto the sink. Startled he picked it up and discovered it was a lipstick. He examined it for a moment and tried to decipher how it got there. Moreover, who did it belong to? Holding it in his hand we went back to the bedroom and sat on his bed. He was baffled with the conundrum at hand. He knew he had been working hard with little time to socialize. It also had been really long since he had brought a woman home. He scratched his head and released a sigh in frustration. He then closed his eyes and … Eureka! His eyes wide-open now in amazement as a rush of blood filled his head. He went back two weeks to the night when Maya first came to his flat, more than tipsy and with a supercilious attitude. He also remembered how he held her tightly in his arms subduing her to tears. He gazed at the lipstick again. He suddenly felt mortified, for being a domineering person was not his trait. He had always been in control of situations even his emotions but controlling someone against her or his will was against his nature. But that day, holding the struggling Maya in his arms, was different. He couldn't say he enjoyed controlling her but he took pleasure in having her close to him. He realized then, he would like to see her again. The death of his girlfriend, his beloved Sheila left him barren of feelings. It was Sheila's death that changed his life completely —changing his name and moving to another city— leaving behind everything he once loved. The immense pain that afflicted him turned him into a stoic person, thus love and romance were non-existent in his life.

Aakash had shielded his heart to protect himself from feeling vulnerable to love. He refused to give in to weakness, the kind that he felt being next to Maya. He knew he was a passionate man capable of giving love, capable of making a woman happy; however he was frightened of being in that situation again. When most guys his age were still figuring out whom they were and what they wanted out of life, Aakash had already been living to the fullest. So, how come now he was feeling like those immature guys? Not knowing what to do regarding his feelings toward Maya. Ever since he met Maya he'd been intrigued. She was neither bold like Priya nor boisterous like Rita. She was reserved, soft spoken and cautious. On the other hand, she had an air of mystery about her he couldn't decipher. Maya hardly spoke to him on their first meeting, except for a few formalities, she had kept to herself. Yet, he couldn't resist wanting to find out more about her. It would torment him unbearably if he didn't satisfy his desire to unveil this mystifying creature who posed as a woman with the soul of a child. Holding the lipstick in his hand, he grinned and promised to himself he would learn more about her as soon as he got back from his trip. Oh, the agony, the sweet surrender that he once knew had returned. Could this be love? Was this an illusion? Was he given a second chance at love? Could he love again? Could he make Maya happy? Could Maya reciprocate his love? Aakash continued with the repertoire of questions as if punishing himself for feeling this way. And with that last question he got up from the bed and threw the lipstick on the floor thinking what a fool he was for indulging in such thoughts. "How naïve of me to think she doesn't have anyone in her life" He said to himself angrily. "A beautiful woman like Maya can't be alone" he continued. "But…what about…so, who was that guy at Soirée?" Aakash inquired. "Was she lying about him? No! It can't be!" He paced back and forth. He picked up the lipstick from the floor and held it in his hand looking at it as if scrutinizing it. "How did I lose composure over a lipstick creating such wretched story?" asked incredulously. Aakash couldn't believe in a matter of minutes he had turned into a jealous imaginary boyfriend. While he went on with his speculative monologue, he heard the second blare of horn from down below realizing it was time to go and keep the commitment with National Geographic.

It was a lazy Sunday for Priya who had neither the need nor any desire to start the day early. Getting up early had never been part of her routine. When she attended the university, she laughed at her friends who constantly reminded her of the popular idiom "the early bird catches the worm," only to find out later in her adult life that her friends were right. Reality was a whole different picture here in Bangalore. Her day began waking up very early as she made her way to work every day. She no longer enjoyed the comforts of home, the close ties with her family, and the outings with her group of friends back in Calcutta. For the past three years here she had to keep busy, be responsible and disciplined in order to survive in the computer hub of Silicon Valley down south. She had to be strong and forget her emotional side to keep up with the rest. She had developed a defense mechanism to get over the loneliness and nostalgia, the terrible pang attacks as she called them she occasionally had when she missed her family and her friends. Getting used to a different office setup, living by herself, making new friends needed a lot of foresight, confidence and courage. It was more than a desire for Priya to prove people back home that she could make it without their help. She hated to be pitied, thus she showed her determination by moving away. But most importantly she had to attest she didn't need any sympathy from the man that left her at the altar.

It took her one year to settle down and one more to count the runaway groom as a blessing in disguise. So given the busy schedule she had in Bangalore she treasured Sunday as a day to lavish herself. A day set aside to do nothing at all, a day for leisure, of herbal teas, organic meals, long aromatic baths, as she sauntered around the house in a white bathrobe listening to soft music. She also liked meeting with her colleagues now turned friends or her fiancé Dhiraj whenever he was in town from his business trips. Sometimes she spent the greater part of the day with her dear beautician, Geetha. So today was one of those sluggish Sundays when she had no reason to get out of bed but to loll in the white comfortable pillows and matching white duvet. Unfortunately, her idle Sunday was over as she received a text message from Rita. Priya was deeply concerned when she learned her friend had some bad news or gut feeling as she put it and asked her to call her as soon as possible. "Oh no, not again!" said Priya, "Poor Rita, she really wanted this affair with Gaurav to blossom into a serious relationship." She didn't hold Gaurav in high regard, but then he was to be Rita's bundle of trouble and not hers. Priya had to be strong for her friend; she had to find the right words to console her in this sad moment. Priya knew this too well since she experienced pain and disappointment when her relationship ended.

Forty minutes later with a mug of black coffee in her hands, Priya was still toying with the approach of broaching the news. Should she just go ahead and give it to her over the phone? Or break it gently on their next ladies night? Better yet, why not have Maya do it? This was becoming a predicament that she definitely didn't want to deal with on a Sunday morning. Her indulging day was over. To make matters worse it was going to be her who broke the bad news and not Rita. She felt guilty for not telling her earlier; Rita was entitled to the truth and she had hid it from her. Priya recalled the day she suggested to have Gaurav checked out. Although Rita thought it was a crazy idea, Priya meant it with the best of intentions, to avoid …well…this mess that was about to unveil. Needless to say, she was right from the beginning to dislike him, for he turned out to be a hypocrite and a scoundrel. The thought of Gaurav having a pregnant wife at home made him more despicable in Priya's eyes. How could he do that to his wife and Rita? She asked herself. The temptation of the flesh was what had trapped Rita in its snare. No need to really toy with mincing words or possible ways to reveal such hurtful truth. She decided to have both Rita and Maya over for coffee and tell them everything. As she let out a sigh of relief, she remembered the note Maya had left for her saying that she was visiting her students and did not know when she will be back. There goes my plan, now what? She thought miserably. Now the onus was on her alone to do the dirty work. She was against the whole idea of crossing the limits of the student-teacher relationship. She would have discouraged her entirely, if she had known before Maya left. Priya didn't approve of Maya's decision since she could be jeopardizing her position as a teacher and ruining her reputation. "Really, Maya can be a bit too naïve at times." Priya said placing her hands on her waist. "She amazes me sometimes. How could she afford to remain so even after everything she's been through?" She went on to say a little resentful. "How did I get myself into this mess? I have problems of my own to solve." Priya protested with annoyance. "Maybe a talk with her is also necessary." Added Priya. She couldn't grasp Maya's reasoning for attending this meeting that only meant a step away from trouble. She knew so little about these students; where they really came from, what their family values were, their ideologies, etc. They were here to study; far away from home with no parental supervision and with so much freedom. For these students being away from home must be heaven and the fact they were in Bangalore even better. Unlike Calcutta, and even other parts of southern India, Bangalore is much less conservative.

Rita had just finished dressing up when Priya called her to invite her over for coffee. She accepted happily. She had no plans for this evening since Gaurav said he was busy attending his family business. She would have loved to meet him today, and spend the entire day hugging him, cuddling and making love to him, doing all the things couples in love usually do. She fantasized on how the entire day would have worked out to their enjoyment. Rita continued daydreaming how she would have cooked breakfast and lunch for both followed by a session of love-making or sex as he used to put it, then a nap and some more love-making. However, the day before he announced Sunday was impossible for him. He made up some excuses and finally told her he could not take her to his flat because of the nosey landlord. Moreover, family engagements promised to keep him busy throughout the day and there was no way of getting out of them. She thought this attitude to be a little selfish on his part. She couldn't fathom the importance of such engagements. She reflected upon this for a minute and decided to be a bit more understanding. After all, he took care of all her needs and put up with her idiosyncrasies such as her monophobia or fear of being alone, shopping addiction and high tendency to alcoholism. He took her to the snazzy nightclubs and bought her clothes and perfumes. All these topped by great sex, maybe a little too much but she was not complaining. He even tolerated that high-browed babe, Priya who thought no end of herself, and demanded a lot of patience on his part. Could she not be then just a little reasonable? She was a little too clingy, she conceded.

Ever since the day she met Gaurav at People's Bank when she went to enquire about the check that had not cleared after 35 days, she had taken to him as a duck takes to water. He went out of his way to enquire at their Mumbai branch and got it all processed. As a gesture of gratitude and more as a means to get to know him better, she suggested going for coffee. He accepted not once but all the times she asked him. He was charming and easy to talk to. He showered her with compliments any woman would have loved. They had lengthy conversations that could have gone on for hours had it not been for time constraint. She started calling him on his direct line, which made her happy when she learned he never gave out this number. Little by little he started inviting her to nightclubs, and she in return to all the parties her friends organized. Among other things they shared their love for a fast-paced life with big doses of clubbing, partying and drinking D2 (d square) as they called it. She was proud to display him the way an artist exhibits his masterpiece. She was aware of his beauty and so was everybody else. Soon she became the envy of her colleagues. Rita couldn't understand then why Priya was just too critical of her and later suggested to have him checked out. Honestly, she was happy with this man and even if he had flaws she was ready to accept them. Her only complaint was that she knew nothing about his family and she certainly felt entitled to make their acquaintance. However, he avoided the subject every time she mentioned them by making up stories such as he had a terrible childhood, almost traumatic; he was estranged from them, lived alone and was trying to put all those memories behind. He always told her all he cared about and wanted in life was her. Sometimes he would change the subject by kissing her, seducing her or talking about sex; something they had no problem talking about. He knew this was one of Rita's weaknesses and he used it well. Rita questioned why talking about sex, which is sometimes considered a taboo was easier to handle than talking about his family. She rationalized love was all about understanding, patience and giving. So far, Gaurav had been doing all the giving and she hadn't reciprocated accordingly. Was this love she felt for him? She repeatedly asked herself. And if it was, then she wanted to pursue it for it was great what she felt being next to him.

In the kitchen, Priya was preparing the coffee and setting a tray with pastries. In a small vase she put wild flowers: Nilam, or Floss flower and some violets. Rita was a little nervous, feeling countless accusations looming her way. Sitting across her and reading her expression, Rita had a sinking feeling that began in her heart and went down to the pit of her stomach. She felt butterflies in her stomach and a cold sweat transpiring from her hands as she could almost hear Priya reproaching her for not listening to her advice. Hence, she tried to brace herself for the storm and keep a straight face. But what she heard from Priya's mouth surpassed everything she had imagined a man could do to the woman he professed love. "I am so sorry my dear" Priya said looking down. "Believe me, I didn't want to be the bearer of such news" went on Priya. Rita was silent and in a state of disbelief. She always thought she could sense trouble miles away due to her experience with her previous relationships. She had dated conceited, self-centered and apathetic men who wanted a fling, a short lived relationship, with no commitments of any kind. The majority of these men share one characteristic: none wanted marriage. All these setbacks had not bothered Rita before, but this now; this was a blow to her face. She would have bet a lot of money, her life even about her previous boyfriends turning out to be losers but Gaurav was different.

Now she understood the reason for his secretive behavior and pretexts that surrounded him every time they brought up the family subject. Rita clasped her hands and rubbed them hard as if trying to cleanse the sinful hands that touched that adulterer. She had a higher opinion of him since he was a serious professional, a great colleague and friend, an excellent lover and last but not least, an attentive listener. In her eyes now he was no better than the losers she had dated before; even worse, he was an irresponsible and a liar. How could he make a mockery of marriage? How could he disrespect his wife and his family? Didn't his vows mean anything to him? Rita was appalled at the thought of this. After hearing the extent of Gaurav's deceit, this issue as painful as it was became hazy and unimportant. All that mattered to her then was how not to break down before Priya. She wanted to make herself disappear and find her way home at once. Somehow she mustered the necessary strength to get up from the chair and managed to thank Priya for her insight, which saved her from making a further mockery of herself in the months to come.

It was a bright Monday morning in Bangalore, like most mornings here during summer. Unlike her regular schedule, today Maya had something else to do: she was going to sign the contract for the rental house she found. This was another big step in her life. She could finally consider herself an independent woman away from her family, her ex-husband and Priya. She had set some distance with her parents after her divorce and even more now that she lived in Bangalore. She called them once a week as a courtesy but this had not improved their precarious relationship that rooted since the day of her wedding. Her parents felt betrayed when she announced defiantly she was to marry Avik with or without their consent. She disregarded their pleas and reminded them it was her prerogative to choose whomever she pleased for husband. Her subsequent divorce after three years proved them right making their already frail bond more vulnerable. After her divorce Maya was plagued with constant reproaches from her parents reminding her the infinite times they warned her about Avik. She couldn't help but feel guilty for they were right and were at liberty to do so. They made sure to mention she was now a divorcee, which carried a stigma in their society. It was hard enough to find a decent and responsible man nowadays and even worse for a divorced woman. All that, coupled with her unemployed status had made her question the futility of her existence. She even came close to committing suicide a couple of times. A big web of disappointment starting with the loss of her unborn child, then the dissolution of her marriage, the lack of any job to fall back upon had totally grinded her self-esteem. Drowning in despair, Maya accepted her friend's offer to go down to Bangalore for a while even though, she felt guilty for not having kept in touch with her in a long time. She was so grateful to Priya for supporting her and pushing her beyond her limits to overcome her ill-fated past. Maya did not want to ruin their friendship by staying longer plus it would be retrograde on her part fearing she might not have the courage later to move out.

She got inspired when she saw her students who were younger than her and yet so independent. Being a Bengali had its demerits amidst all the goodness she reasoned. For instance, children are always considered children even when they are grown up, thus making them unable to be more independent. Self-reliance in any form is not taught to them. She knew it was part of her culture yet she condemned it. However, there are exceptions to the rule, other parts of India practice better judgment and foresight in bringing up their youngsters, where both girls and boys are equally applauded when they excel and act more maturely. As she started developing her new-found sense of independence in Bangalore, her fear of loneliness diminished and her self-esteem grew stronger. Ravi, her house broker called her on Sunday to inform her of a listing for a house that he liked. He sounded very optimistic about it and said it was perfect for her. He described it as small and cozy and most importantly at a reasonable price considering how high the market value was. It belonged to an elderly couple, who wanted a female non-local resident. The only drawback was that it was far from central Bangalore, in a place called Isro Layout.

So today, before going to college she was going to meet her broker to check out the house. They met at 9:00 a.m. and reached their destination about forty minutes later. They entered the two-story house and she liked what she saw at first glance. It was cozy indeed; it had a bedroom, a bathroom, a big double-usage room as kitchen and dining room plus a small den that she could use as a living room. To her luck, she was delighted to find she had exclusive access to the roof where it served as a terrace. Twenty minutes later, Maya thanked both Ravi and Mr. Murlidharan, her future landlord and scheduled an appointment for Wednesday to finalize the contract and give her down payment. Having accomplished one more real life task she headed happily towards college. On her way up she met Mrs. Lalli, the lead professor who was Bengali. In the short time Maya had been working at the college they established a good friendship. Maya felt immense satisfaction knowing that she was learning to open up to people without being apprehensive, thus giving herself a chance to make friends. Maya was so elated with her news she wanted to share them with Mrs. Lalli. In the elevator, on her way to class she told her about her fortunate finding. Lalli hugged her and congratulated her insisting they should celebrate. "Let's go to the pub next door tonight." Lalli said enthusiastically. "I am sorry Lalli, not today. Do you want to take a rain check? I promise to do it some other time, but tonight I have to call my father to ask him for the down payment I have to give on Wednesday." "Oh come on, you can call him from my house." Lalli said putting her hand on Maya's shoulder. Maya tried to evade the invitation as she didn't want to inconvenience her friend. "Just wait for me after class. Don't run off, ok? See you later" said Lalli and entered her class. "Ok, bye" was all that Maya could manage.

Maya headed toward her classroom and as she walked down the hall she looked through the window at the busy road that lay below, snaking its way toward the eastern part of Bangalore. Maya breathed in all the activity she saw from above. The college was next to the busy intersection called Richmond Circle, where cars, rickshaws and Karnataka state buses hustled. She found out later this intersection was nicknamed Suley Circle as it was commonly referred to by the auto-wallas,(the drivers). On the opposite side of the road facing Maya was the All Saints Bakery, which was also a small shop, strategically located in a booming part of town. She could see people from all walks of life. Looking from above, they all looked the same, she concluded...but then...she spotted some of her students who were wearing their beautiful bright-colored garments rushing to class and she smiled. They too look the same, she thought. Maya wondered how she had missed this revealing sight while trying to maintain discipline in the classroom and forgetting to look out the window for a moment. She realized life didn't stop and went on no matter how big her problem was. There was a world to explore out there. Maya reveled in this moment of awareness, both as an outsider observing the intricacies and the fallibilities of human existence and also on a personal level, as Maya with all her failures and accomplishments.

As planned earlier, Maya accepted Lalli's invitation and after work the women headed for Gandhi Nagar where Lalli lived. Maya immediately called Priya to let her know she was coming late. It turned out that Priya had plans as well. She informed her Dhiraj was in town therefore she was going to come home late. Maya was relieved because she didn't want to rush home; she wanted to enjoy Lalli's hospitality. Besides, Lalli told her she was happy to have her over because these days she didn't have much company. Then Maya called her father to let him know she had found a place and needed to give the down payment on Wednesday. Her father promised to transfer the funds to her account and asked her not to withdraw any money from her savings account. Since he couldn't convince her to stay in Calcutta or dissuade her from going to Bangalore he decided to help her behind her mother's back. Maya was pleased to have her father's support at a time like this. While Maya was on the phone talking to her father, Lalli was in the kitchen preparing some drinks and appetizers. Maya felt comfortable in Lalli's company. Besides indulging in serious topics, the two women shared a good laugh along with some gossips who served as a stress reliever after a long day at work. They had a couple of drinks and shared personal memoirs. Lalli was also excited to introduce someone from her city to her husband. They lived on the second floor of an apartment building and the moment Maya stepped into their flat it reminded her of her student's place.

At first glace, she couldn't see Lalli's decoration style anywhere in the apartment. The interior decoration definitely had a Persian motif from the furniture to the thick Persian carpet covering the floor. Even the smell that pervaded the room was not Indian. It had neither the coconut smell —reminiscent of a typical southern Indian household— neither the aroma of cloves, cinnamon, cardamom of the great mix of the Indian spice, nor the strong fish smell of a Bengali house. Instead it had a strong smell of garlic and some mysterious herbs. They had prepared a dish of rice called Taadi and a meaty dish with vegetables called Gurma-sabzee. The rice was oily and fried —the part they most relished was the hard, brown rice grains stuck at the bottom of the pan— and topped with a pickle called Torshi, which was all garlic. Of course, she gathered all the details later while eating, which was quite a late dinner. Needless to say, the entire gourmet experience was prepared by Abbas, Lalli's husband. He was fair-skinned and good looking, with a stout body that was apparent through the white T-shirt that he was wearing. The whole atmosphere was splendid; the unusual yet appetizing smell from the kitchen, heart-rending Persian music that filled the air with mysticism plus Persian décor transported Maya to Iran. Over dinner they joked about the difference between Iranian and Indian men. Lalli was blatantly expressive while describing how good the Iranian husbands are, as a partner, a companion, and in bed. Maya felt embarrassed listening to Lalli banter on about the sexual prowess of Abbas and how they could put the author of Kama Sutra to shame with the variety that they practiced in bed. Lalli was laughing and enjoying Maya's blushed face as she told these stories. Lalli was also enjoying the opportunity to speak in her mother tongue with Maya since she didn't have anyone else to do so. However, she was still a good hostess and made sure Maya was served dessert —a bowl of dry fruits, a plate full of toffees, small chocolates to go along with drinks— in the customary way. Maya made a mental note of the fact that unlike Indians they had fruits, often the juicy variety as an accompaniment to hard liquor.

Since Maya was not so much into drinking and going by her last experience, she settled for a glass of vodka, only after a lot of persuasion from Lalli. Actually, it was a vodka based drink called Aarrakh —a bluish and very sweet drink— deceptively potent as she found out later. Maya paid the price yet again of having two Aarrakh drinks. Luckily, she was at Lalli's home hence, not too much damage was done. She was still able to carry on a conversation that revolved around their students and the college. So deciding to share their hospitality further, Lalli asked Maya to stay over since it was too late for her to go back home alone. Maya retired to their guest room and even before she could look around the room and go through the evening in her mind as was her habit, she slipped unceremoniously into a deep sleep. Maya woke with a loud banging on the door and realized in a matter of minutes that it was still a weekday that meant she had to go to work. Soon after she remembered she was not at Priya's home so her usual routine had to be rearranged. She also had to check with the bank to make sure she had the money deposited from her father's account. Two hours later and a class under her belt she went to the teacher's lounge to get a cup of black coffee. While she sat, she reminisced of the recent events that had emerged in her life. She gathered some strength and went back to the classroom as she still had three more classes before she could head home. She took an auto and arrived home. As she entered the house she received the much awaited call from her father, stating the money was in her account, and could be withdrawn. They talked for a while and Maya excitedly shared with her father the many accomplishments she had recently. Talking with her father again made her feel even more secure. She thanked her father and hung up the phone.

Priya in the meantime found herself in a dilemma. Dhiraj had told her not to expect him any time soon since his business dealings were going to take longer. So it was a surprise indeed when he called her Monday night to let her know he was in Bangalore. A few days earlier, her parents had called her while en route to Tirupathi expressing their desire to pay her a visit. She agreed and was happy to have them over since it had been a long time they hadn't seen each other. She needed to feel again that sense of security that only parents can offer. She could enjoy their company and a week of pampering. As meticulous as she was she immediately planned out a seven-day itinerary for them and a flexible schedule that would permit her to work out of home without compromising her job. Dhiraj's unannounced arrival meant rescheduling her itinerary to one that could fit her parents, her fiancé and her job. At least she had one thing in her favor; she didn't expect her parents until the weekend. Now she had to tackle yet another problem. Where would they sleep? She had a two-bedroom flat and Maya was already using one of the bedrooms.

Forty minutes later after Dhiraj's call, she was sitting at Café Corner sipping coffee and listening to a medley of remixed old songs blaring out from the speakers that hung from the pillars. Café Corner was located on MG Road in the Trade Centre close to Priya's office.

Leaving things half done, she decided to meet Dhiraj here after receiving his sudden call. Although this was not their usual rendezvous joint, it was the most convenient for both of them as he was to pick her up and take her to a special place. She was amazed to see him arrive in his father's car. She pestered him with a line of questions he refused to answer. She was starting to get annoyed when he finally pulled up in front of a cluster of houses somewhere in Jaya Nagar. Dhiraj knew just when to draw the line with Priya and decided not to tempt his fate any longer. Holding her hand he said:

"Relax dear, don't be mad at me. Thanks for bearing with me so patiently. I wanted to surprise you."

"Well that you have! I don't know what I am doing here standing in front of a building" said Priya a little too testily.

"Hey! I thought you would be happy to see me" said Dhiraj a little crestfallen. "Yes, I am, but I could do with less of a prelude! Frankly what are we doing here?" asked Priya.

"You see, I want you to meet my family, actually my father wants to meet you" said Dhiraj and looked at Priya intently to see her reaction. "What? Why didn't you tell me all this before? You just got me irritated and spoiled my mood. Really, I must look like one ill-tempered, tired and grouchy bitch. You men just don't know what to do when!" said Priya angrily and drew the compact out of her bag.

She began frantically fixing her looks and her hair. Five minutes later she regained her composure and was in control of the situation. "But dear you look good, you always do. My father will just love you, so stop worrying" he said and was rewarded with a single "hmmmph" from her. "Women! We can never win!" Thought Dhiraj. More than a little nervous, Priya followed Dhiraj to his house.

In the year they had been dating they had not come here before. They had always met at either some party, gathering or at Priya's place. He would often spend two to three days at a time when he was in town and it was during that time that both realized the need for a bigger place. It was this situation that had prompted Priya to find that place in Cox Town, where they intended to move in together. She had always wondered about his brother and his father, what kind of people were they, how typically Punjabi were they, being so far away from Hariyali of Punjab. In spite of her anxiety, half-hour later the scene inside the flat was of such animated conviviality that she forgot she was at her future father-in-law's place. It was an inviting sight that a stranger would have thought it was the perfect family picture. She sure was glad to know she was about to join a woman-less family. The affair ended with Priya's promise to bring her parents the following Wednesday night for dinner. Mr. Talwar seemed pleased and happy to be a father-in-law soon.

Aakash checked his watch and saw that for the last forty minutes he had been trying to sleep, unsuccessfully. Thousands of miles away from Bangalore, from Maya things went mentally haywire for him ever since he found the wretched lipstick in his pocket and sleep seemed to evade him. What was it doing in his pocket? He remembered last seeing it in the medicine cabinet back at his house. He recounted the events and… of course…he recalled he was sitting on his bed holding the lipstick in his hand when Anil came to pick him up. Instead of throwing it in the waste basket, he had put it in his pocket. He had sworn not to get emotionally attached to another woman, yet here he was in Himachal Pradesh, high up in the mountain trying to untangle his reasoning from his feelings. The truck driver mentioned something to him as they ascended but his mind was in Bangalore and was not able to respond. The part of the documentary dealing with the transportation of tea by road including the life of his driver was only half done. This lifestyle that epitomized simplicity in thought and action was being done in parts and would be finished when they reached Calcutta. Truck loads of tea are transported from the hilly terrain of Himachal to the Gangetic West Bengal —the hub of tea marketing— in a four to five day trip. Aakash was not just pleased doing the entire documentary on the tea production; he also wanted to include the side that nobody talks about, the simplicity and trusting nature that rule the life of these workers. Hence, he was determined to make the driver and his family a part of this project. He wanted to throw light on the inconsequential, over-worked, malnourished workers that made a meager living and were just happy to have a job. Aakash was moved by their resilience and will. He could see a kind of integrity and benevolence that lacked in the typical city dweller. To implement this part of the project he and Anil had to stay with his family in their small cottage. The humble quarters already offered shelter to the driver, his wife, two children and elderly parents, leaving not much room for the two film-makers.

The unassuming dwelling was made of wood and stone, the walls that served as foundations were not plastered and the inside had no dividing walls. Thus, to create divisions they placed saris and sometimes chaddars (bed spreads) over ropes zigzagging all across. The toilet, which was a small make-shift outhouse, was located a few meters away from the house. So in the front part of the cottage both he and Anil were in the midst of the maze of these zigzagging screens. Luckily for him, he had the side next to a small window through which he could just catch a glimpse of the sky, the light of the waning moon and the top of the trees facing the cottage. He could hear the leaves rustling in the wind, the sound of crickets and the chirping of nocturnal birds. It was almost surreal, thought Aakash. The sound of night was so strange, so new, yet omnipresent. Here, at this moment, everything had its place, its own presence, its sound, its own identity. It was odd that among all these people in the cottage he found himself lonely yet at peace. Far away from the known peripheries and comforts of city life the only thing that came between him and nature was Maya. As much as he wanted to see Maya, his work was far from being over, at least three days worth shooting and documenting in Himachal Pradesh and then Calcutta, the final destination of the tea laden trucks. From here all the way to the tea board in Poddar Court for the auction of tea. This meant a minimum of seven days if not more of unbearable and obligatory separation. The intensity of this desire paled his love for his dead Sheila. In retrospect, he now considered that childish affliction of the heart a tragic infatuation. He didn't love Sheila any less for he still cherished her memory. He justified it as a stark difference in the Puneet of those days, and today's Aakash. He had matured over the years and outgrown the idealisms of youth becoming more practical and realistic, a much seasoned and resilient version. Deep down inside he was still the old Puneet, yet with a marked new entity. It was this new entity that sought Maya and could only find fulfillment of spirit in her arms.

PART II

Seven days had passed since she moved out of Priya's place and into her own; at least a flat she could call her own. Hardly furnished and far from being comfortable, the sparse rooms cried out for adornments. A very austere setting, these rooms were a far cry from those she had inhabited before during her single years and then as the wife of Avik. In the three years of her marital life with Avik, her small but comfortable flat had been her pride which she tastefully decorated. In defiance to the dullness in her marriage she redecorated it with bright hue draperies and cushions such as bright orange, gold and red. The Gujrati hand-stitched pillow covers with Zarree border and the quilt gave a unique look to the bed. Bronze figurines of different shapes and sizes added the touch of contemporary style and bespoke of her love for the folk art of Bengal and Murshidabad. The two figurines of horses made out of burnt clay supporting the typical workmanship of Bankura —a district in Bengal— found its place in the dining area. Her passion for reading was reflected in the overloaded shelves and coffee tables extending it to their nightstand; even the bathroom window sill was not spared. Her experimentation with indoor gardening, revealed itself in the huge green and yellow striped healthy leaves of the Money plant in the kitchen, in the living room and also in the bedroom.

All that and much more, she left behind after the divorce. She felt a huge sense of loss when she took one more look at her nicely decorated flat. All those ornaments had filled her life with pleasure, the one Avik never provided. A sudden flashback of all those painful memories zoomed across her mind as she admired her new place, and she was certainly glad those memories were buried in the past. Standing in the middle of the empty room made her realize she was lonelier than before here in Bangalore except when she sought refuge in her thoughts. She appreciated the time she lived with Priya as she was her companion during her difficult transition. However, the onus of finding the true identity of Maya Ghosal lay within herself. She had been a good daughter, sister, cousin, friend, student and wife. All that had been stripped from her as she became part of Avik's family. Her in-laws tried to shame her and drag her through the mud but she never lost hope that one day she would triumph over all their pettiness. Indeed, she rose like the phoenix and more than ever she was determined to regain her merits. She was Maya Ghosal, the woman known to all as worthy of any man, intelligent, independent and capable of loving.

Self discovery can be fun at times when you are sitting in the college cafeteria with your friends and sharing many things: cups of tea, gossips, heartaches, and personality traits. In the confines of these public rooms amidst one's friends, only the good qualities and highly aspired moralities surfaced, to please the self and others as they came out naturally sometimes and other times projected, she observed. The person that showed compassion, higher intellect, and overall cleverness was always looked upon respectfully and was the center of attention, adulation, even envy. Sometimes it was essential to possess at least one of those qualities to be accepted by friends. Maya qualified as a spectator for she had always been the bashful type. She listened and wondered, but never questioned, sometimes she admired others from the back seat and sometimes she was appalled but in spite of it all, she never joined to unmask or glorify the inner self.

Maya Ghosal possessed the qualities that matched the more conservative, northern Calcutta upbringing. Then again being the Didi or the older sister to brother Nikhil, she had her own responsibilities, and code of conduct to follow. Maya needed to fulfill certain expectations from society but she never had to figure herself out as everything had already been figured out for her. But now it was different, her present situation demanded her to take notice of this new person that had emerged from the turbulence of past circumstances. Sitting all alone in these empty rooms, she was face to face with herself. Her past, her present, her future, her fears and doubts all staring at her waiting to be explored. She had to confront now what she avoided all her young adult life: herself. Who could she confide in? Was it better to ignore her painful past? Could she deal with the present without healing the wounds of her past? Was she really ready to move forward? Her head started spinning with the sound of her own recriminations. Her new status of divorced woman was easier to bear than all the unanswered questions she had.

Priya, her sweet friend from the good old university days had gone through hardships as well. But this new metamorphosed Priya was much different as far as emotions and convictions were considered. Naturally, she had created a defense mechanism that would help her survive in her new city. She was determined to succeed and put her doubts and disappointments behind. Priya seemed well-adjusted. She always seemed sure of herself and at times a bit haughty. Maya almost dared to say her friend was hardened by the misfortune that haunted her until her arrival in Bangalore. She thought Priya had become apathetic in order to endure the trials of life. Maya wondered if this type of change was even positive as it could impede her personal growth and development as a person. But Maya was not Priya, she reflected. Her heart had not hardened yet, she acknowledged she was still fearful and shy. Every day, here in Bangalore was a battle for her, where she had to struggle by putting on a mask before stepping out of her home. The real Maya remained hidden behind self-doubt while the superficial Maya faced the world. She felt uncomfortable with this pretense as she never considered herself a two-faced individual. Sometimes she blamed her parents for raising her in a conservative household, a little sheltered from the world, a little too self-conscious, in order to conform to the rules of society. She wanted to blame everybody but herself for having a feeble personality that was not compatible with today's world.

As a teacher and a role model to her students, Maya set her feelings and personal problems aside. She would never drag her beloved students in her sorrows much less invite them to see that gloomy side of her. In fact, it was her students who gave her a reason to smile and forget her grief. Therefore, she was infinitely grateful to them for she had not smiled in a long time. She concealed her fears and never showed the downcast Maya; instead she personified courage and self-confidence. She later realized she had become an expert in her ability to live a dual existence: the bold Maya at work and the anxious scared little girl at home. She also acknowledged her growing desire to keep afloat amidst all her complexities. It all came down to acceptance she asserted once as she recalled her gatherings in the university cafeteria. Her friends were looking to be accepted by others. Her parents comply with the conformities of society, thus looking for acceptance as well. Not a lot has changed since then, she thought. Wasn't it true she sought approval from Avik's family? Didn't she want acceptance from her parents too? Is it any different now? She wanted to be accepted by her students, colleagues, Priya and even Aakash. How could she be recognized by the world if her biggest enemy, herself, wouldn't accept her as she was? In order to do so she had to absolve Maya of her faults.

She needed a few basic things and furniture to fill in the space, not seeking luxury but seeking comfort. Just the day before, she had seen a supermarket called The Cosmos, while returning from college. She went in and quickly browsed the items they had making a mental note to shop there for her essential household products. The huge boards of Ugadi[6] Special also convinced her she made a wise decision. Once she arrived home while she was paying the auto driver she wrote down the pronunciation of the Kannada[7] word Kathrigruppe, the name of the neighborhood where the supermarket was, in case she forgot it and could not pronounce it correctly to the driver next time she went. She was so motivated and enthusiastic about going shopping for her new place she returned the next day armed with a shopping list. The immensity of the place with the assortment of merchandise was too overwhelming and she was soon lost in the sea of brands and labels. Rows and rows of various displays confused her as she stood surrounded by items, signs and a crowd of people. They had a wide variety of goods that surpassed her expectations. It was the type that had flooded and conquered the Indian retail market in a surge of department stores. She was so entertained breathing in the liveliness of this moment she had forgotten she was Maya, the

---

[6]*Ugadi literally the start of an era. Is the new year's day of the people of the Deccan region of India. While the people of Andhara Pradesh and Karnataka use the term Ugadi for the festival. It is celebrated on different day every year because the Hindu calendar is a lunisolar calendar.*

[7]*Is one of the major Dravidian languages of India, spoken predominantly in the southern state of Karnataka. It is the 27th most spoken language in the world numbering roughly 35 million and it is one of the official languages of India.*

stranger from Calcutta trying to make her way in Bangalore. She paid attention to people's comments especially to the women who knew where the good sales were exclaiming 'exciting offer' pronounced in the typical southern Indian accent as exziting offer, that was going on there because of Ugadi. She found herself in the middle of a swirl of languages such as English, Kannada and even in Tamil.

Ugadi is the celebration of the New Year in the state of Karnataka, and true to the occasion, there was a festival, hence the discount on items, special offers and total frenzy. It was such an exquisite sight, the sweet chaos of the holiday. Women were busy weighing the possibilities of better deals with better items, as they paused and pulled at the huge tins of Ghee, or the extra large packet of tamarind, or that extra heavy sack of sugar, and the finest of Basmati rice. The picturesque scene was further enhanced with the sea of saris from the south, Chennai silks, Bangalore and Kanjeepuram silks. Most of the women she saw there had long black curly hair they wore either loose or braided, but all adorned with single or multiple strands of Chameli, Jasmine and some orange flower unknown to her. The smell of these flowers along with the hair oils of jasmine, coconut, along with the general smell of groceries and Temple dhoop (incense), created an aura that was authentically southern and quite unlike anything she experienced before.

Indeed, life was nice and kind, almost as caring as a mother –she knew just when to be tough or gentle and when to deprive or give. The year had run its half course and she was already flooded with new information of so many kinds. While on one hand, she was trying to acclimatize her ear to the phonetics of Kannada and Tamil as well as to manners and ways of these gentle, helpful Karnataka people, on the other hand she was spending seven hours with her Iranian students at the college. It was through them that she would often glimpse far off —Iran the land of mystery and beauty— at least to her, and hitherto unknown to her. Maya was a romantic fool by nature, thus she was totally biased in their favor due to their tender and gentle spirit. Completing the shopping expedition in almost two hours, Maya found herself once again in her newly acquired flat with her load of broom, mop, bucket and several small plastic jars and assortment of kitchen items, along with many packets of semi cooked food. Coming back home from the market had been quite an experience in itself, but she had felt a huge sense of accomplishment and pride. She decided she would add and place the mats and covers on Sunday, plus the small items she had also bought to decorate her flat. Once the barren room was somewhat furnished she would give a small housewarming party, she thought. Feeling totally satisfied, she lay down on the bed and closed her eyes to rest a while.

Unlocking the door of his flat, Aakash headed straight to the bathroom. Even before doing anything else, he went to relieve himself and wash away the grime and dust off his body. So just dropping the shoulder bag in the living room, he tore off his shirt and jeans, threw his sunglasses on his bed along with his watch and entering the bathroom turned the shower full blast. Twenty minutes later, wrapped in his grey bathrobe and feeling more like his usual self he started shaving the grown beard. Enveloped in the musky smell of his favorite soap, he brushed his hair backwards and sat on his bed. Ever since his work had finished at the tea auction in Calcutta, he felt a gnawing excitement, building slowly and then spreading like wild fire all over him, of just being back in the same city, where soon he would meet Maya. He could also sense an impending doom if he failed to meet her and express his true feelings. Life had cheated him once from being happy next to Sheila so he was not going to let that happen again. His normally calm and confident self did not feel invincible anymore; instead he felt pitiful and nervous like a young boy, not like the thirty-six year old man he was. What better way then to initiate his plan by calling Maya? He would invite her out with the pretext of returning the lipstick –the originator that had stirred up his dormant feelings. He was suddenly excited at the idea of meeting her soon "Yes, that's it!" He exclaimed with a triumphant voice followed by a "Damn it!" as he realized he lacked a piece of vital information, her telephone number. He flipped open his cellular phone and called Priya at once. He was even happier that he had managed to get Maya's number without giving any explanations to Priya. He feared Priya's inquisitive nature, but fortunately for him she just informed him she had recently bought a cellular phone. He didn't lose any time and before pressing the green icon on the left side of his cellular to generate the call and start a new chapter in his life, he looked at his watch to confirm the conduciveness of the day and time to go ahead. It was one o'clock, lunch time it seemed just right; he pressed it and waited patiently hearing the rings. She must be having lunch or napping perhaps, he thought. In fact a nap in the afternoon went with her personality. She seemed laid back and a homebody, he assumed thinking she would always start her day unhurriedly taking pleasure in everything she did. So well conjured was the picture of her in his mind that he did not mind the unanswered rings, as he imagined Maya in all stages of waking up from the afternoon nap she was indulging in. However, he did not have to wait too long, for Maya soon said:

"Hello?"

"Am I speaking to Maya?" He asked.

"Yes, who is this?" asked Maya even though she had an uncanny feeling about who the caller might be and as if in response, her body froze. Could it really be?

"This is Aakash here … I know it's bit of a surprise … but still …" he said slowly trying to be cautious as if measuring everything he said.

"Oh hi, but how did you get my number? Nobody but few …" Maya trailed off. "Well, that was the easiest part. Anyway, I called because I want to return a thing to you, something that belongs to you."

"Mine? Impossible!" she felt irritated, but toned down quickly as she realized that she was in the teachers' lounge and met the curious eyes of one colleague as she looked up from the sandwich she was eating. Getting up and going toward the window with her back towards the solitary colleague, she repeated into the cellular

"How can that be? I left as soon I got up!"

"What? You didn't even read the note I left for you?" He said teasing her.

"Well, I did as instructed and kept the key under the mat and left, so I don't know what I could have dropped behind." She replied.

"Hmm, that you did, it would be interesting to know if you are always so obedient … but enough about that …" said Aakash.

"Obedient? Excuse me!" said Maya flaring up.

"Come on now, no need to get all that excited, tell me, should I come to your place now or do you want me to pick you up somewhere?" he asked in a placating voice. "Now is impossible because I am not at home" said she smugly.

"Why, where are you? Asked Aakash a little irritated.

"It seems you are unaware of the fact that I am working these days and I'm busy," said she with immense pleasure, "… therefore you can't meet me."

"I can, and I will, just give me the address I will be there."

"You are not getting the point, are you? I'm busy now and will be till 5:00 p.m., and there is no need for you to come" said Maya.

"That is for me to decide, just give me the address" said he with such finality that raised no further argument. Maya was also a bit curious to know what she had left behind, so gave him the address and directions go to get there. A little later, a much toned down Maya, went back to her classes with a lunch half eaten and a head full of questions. The telephone conversation had taken up the rest of her lunch break and now it was time for her last three classes.

Aakash now a happier man went about planning the rest of the day till 4:00 p.m. Only one thing somehow bothered him, the fact he had been wrong picturing a more serene Maya. He still nurtured that loving image of Maya sleeping on his bed, so innocent, so fragile. He couldn't fathom the idea of her working until early evening. He was selfish to believe she was going to be available for him on his sudden whim. A lot had happened in the span of a month indeed. With a smirk on his face, he congratulated himself for having arrived at the realization that he was deeply intrigued and interested in her. He was clear now of what he wanted; he wanted to make her his. He had a strong need to be with her, to understand her, to know her better, but could all this be love? He then analyzed further that for the first time he felt anxious being with a woman. He didn't want to accept this sudden feeling of insecurity as he had always been self-assured. Was this the reason he always teased Maya? Was he projecting his agitation by being mean toward Maya? Was he using sarcasm as a defense mechanism? Since this was a serious and meaningful date after so many years, he wanted to make a good impression. He started rummaging through his wardrobe trying to pick the winning outfit for the right occasion. He was overwhelmed with the task at hand. How could such simple decision turned into a big mission? Feeling defeated after a while, he sat on his bed staring at his once neatly organized closet now upturned like a ship wrecked on a stony shore. Disgusted at this side of his inept personality he finally decided on a pair of faded jeans and a short sleeve, off-white cotton shirt, his Rolex watch and his favorite pair of sunglasses. His slightly long hair made him look like a maverick. Hence, he decided against tying it and keeping the sunglasses perched on his head instead. He splashed a little cologne and left his house.

He reached Brigade Tower at 4:45 p.m. and decided to wait downstairs. Maya kept fidgeting with the pen in her hand and looking at her watch; her last class was about to be finished in the next fifteen minutes. Ever since she spoke to Aakash, she could not concentrate on anything else. Even the practical class, where they did all sorts of exciting things like skits, story telling, role playing or charades, failed to capture and hold her attention today. Her mind was busy spinning the different version of the telephone conversation that she had with Aakash and the possible nuances of his responses. Finally, when it was time to go, she realized that she was nervous for it had been years that she had gone out with a man on a date. She felt mentally and emotionally handicapped to even imagine being in such a situation again, let alone face it. More so, the man in question here was not like any other she had met before. From the few chats she had had with him, it was clear to her that he was not the weak, pathetic, indecisive type who didn't know what he wanted. On the contrary, he appeared to be a man who knew exactly what he wanted, the aggressive type. Maya could read an indication of strong will and dynamic personality in his calm and attractive expression. Maya sensed as only a woman could, his strength of mind and spirit, strict sense of justice and decency. She couldn't deny she was attracted to these alluring traits like moths to a light bulb. Hence, she had maintained all possible distance from him, until this afternoon when he called. Men in general were the last thing she needed at this point in her life and much less someone like him. "Hi, I thought you would be late" said Aakash with a smile "… just to postpone seeing me."

"Why? I am not scared of you" blurted out Maya.

"Scared? No, you got me wrong. I thought I was the dessert you were saving for the last course!" He finished with a wicked gleam in his eyes provoking Maya completely. However, Maya not willing to be drawn in his little game, and right in the presence of her students said instead "Well, where is my thing that you seem to have treasured for so long?"

"Patience my dear, let's go to a decent place first" said he and holding her by the hand directed her towards a waiting auto and got into it. It seemed he had everything figured out and before she could react she found herself in the auto unable to protest. Afraid of what her students might have thought, she avoided making a public scene. She condemned this type of behavior and was one thing that she hated all her life; hence it was the last thing she wanted to do now. Instead, she expressed her protest at his brazen behavior with a steely

- and after that -

glance and a futile effort at twisting her hand out of his hand.

A born introvert and a romantic at heart, striving to find romance in big and small gestures, she was instead constantly caught between crudity and crassness in the behavior of people around her. The insensitivity and pettiness of her relatives and those of Avik tormented her and forced her to regress further into the shell that she created to protect herself. But no shelter could have protected her from the humiliation and the exposure of her divorce. The traumatic experience lay bare to all and sundry –the story of her miserable marriage became a public property with all its opinions, and viewpoints with total fanfare and unsavory finality. So, in spite of her loathing of Aakash's gesture, she pretended it didn't bother her to avoid any manifestation of anger. Sitting opposite him in Café Corner on MG Road she was reasonably calm to feign indifference to his presumptuousness. However, Aakash was undaunted in his gaiety and soon ordered Cappuccino for both of them and drawing the chair closer said "Frankly speaking it was not my intention to return your thing."

"What!! Why then all this … what is your intention then?" Maya asked totally bewildered. In response he simply looked straight at her and in a very calm and soft voice said "To see you." Maya was speechless, for no one had been so straight forward as to admitting that it was her presence they had craved for. Hearing this short and sincere phrase Maya realized how special this meeting had become; how important she had become for him, so much so that he had to make an inane pretext. But bashful Maya could only look away.

"Maya, what happened? Are you that angry you don't want to look at me?" he said tenderly extending his hand and reaching for hers.

Maya now looking down could only feel the strong masculine hand that was caressing her.

"Angry? No, I am just confused" she finally found the courage to say.

"Confused, but why?" Aakash asked surprised.

"Well, for starters you sounded so sweet and nice ... uh ...unlike the overpowering Aakash I have previously seen" said Maya softly, still refusing to look directly at him. "Now listen to me Maya, I know I haven't been, well ... a very charming person and I'm sorry. Can't we be friends?" He asked with a soft look on his face withdrawing his hand from hers.

Forcing a smile, Maya then said "I could try if you promise not to mock me ever again!"

"Mock you? Never, I like to tease you a bit, for you are fun to watch, but not mock. Well, enough of that now. Have you finished your coffee? Let's go somewhere else, it's too loud and crowded, I can hardly hear you." Indeed, as the daylight was giving in to evening darkness, the place was getting crowded by the minute. That, topped with music blaring and a gusty wind blowing intermittently, was making it difficult to carry on a conversation.

"I am sorry but I can't go, I have to head home, it's already seven" said Maya apologetically. Looking at his watch he said "Yes that's right, but isn't your house, rather your friend's house just round the corner?"

"It was, but I moved out" "What? When?" almost screamed Aakash in a sudden burst of surprise.

"About two weeks ..." Maya trailed off.

"But why Maya, so suddenly, what happened? And for goodness

- and after that -

sake who are you staying with?" With so many questions fired at her in rapid succession, she had to look at him and was mildly surprised to see so much emotion surfacing from his otherwise calm face. He seemed really concerned about her, and that was something she did not want. Hence discouraging any such closeness with Aakash she said "Nothing major happened, what is so unusual about it? In any case, everybody does it here."

"You!" he paused menacingly, "are not everybody."

"Well I am not a child either!"

"Nonsense! You are a beautiful but very confused child who thinks is a woman that can take care of herself! You need to move back with your friend at once! He practically growled in one breath.

"Really? You can't change, can you? This bossy and controlling attitude of yours! I have taken enough of it all my life, I can't take it anymore" she declared angrily but instead of feeling the anger rise as expected, her lips suddenly started quivering and tears rolled down out the corners of her eyes. Aakash sat shocked in a state of bewilderment, at Maya's sudden burst of emotion. As he stared at Maya he thought he was right then to think there is a past to her, painful, he was sure; something that tormented her still and had brought her so far away from Calcutta. The possibility of a broken heart over a boyfriend crossed his mind but then she didn't look the type to encourage meaningless relationships, he reasoned. Could it be that she was married? The likelihood of a husband lurking somewhere in her past made him mad as a hornet; yet helpless and hopeless. He experienced a sinking feeling and could feel his palms getting sweaty. God he thought, what did that moron do to her that scarred her psyche? He saw she was trying to keep her composure despite her burst of tears, so he said "Maya please calm down and tell me who are you staying with, and where?" Aakash said, in a voice that was choked with concern.

"I am calm, I am staying alone in Isro Layout" Maya said in a low but calm manner. "What! Alone? Can you really manage dear? You are just a little more than a child?" Aakash said in a soft tone yet not sincere enough for Maya who exasperatingly exclaimed, "Stop patronizing me! For your information I am not your 'dear' and I am definitely not a child!" Maya would have carried on had he not clamped her mouth with his hand.

"Ok Maya, I am sorry. At least let me drop you home" and saying that he released his hand. Maya got up instantly the moment his hand was off her and said "Don't touch me like that again. I can be your friend if and only if you act like a gentleman and not otherwise." Aakash didn't say anything further but vowed silently to take care of her for the rest of their life together. He could almost sense that she was aware of his sentiments and of his fondness and desire for her. Before today, he would have misinterpreted this incident as pride but after the short outbreak, he realized it was her effort at protecting herself from possible hurt, and …. "What happened? Are we not going?" Maya broke in, interrupting his thoughts. In response, Aakash just looked at her and paying off the bill went in search of an auto.

The entire time of their half-hour ride, they didn't speak to one another as each was caught in their respective web of thoughts and fears. However, he caught her glancing at him sideways many times during the ride, and wondered as to what she could be thinking. Maybe she wanted to say something? Possibly she found the silence oppressive. Sitting in the dark, close confines of the auto with her, made him feel almost part of her essence; the brush of her flyaway hair carrying with it the faint smell of shampoo against the side of his face, the whiff of her perfume now in a much different smell mixed with her sweat, had a muskiness that intoxicated him further. He kept quite still breathing in the very core of her being, not wishing it to end. On the other hand, Maya felt that she had to break this silence because there was an uncanny vibration that was disturbing and could prove dangerous. She was keenly aware of him and wished it was not so dark outside so she wouldn't feel uncomfortable being next to him. The night brought out inhibitions as well as ardent passions. The audacity of his deliberate and intense touch — unexpected and brazen, and now his silence—frightened her. Somehow, her ex-husband's touch had never left such an indelible impression on her the way Aakash's did. When not under the influence of his demanding mother, Avik was sweet; however those moments were as rare as not worth counting. He was very predictable in all his moods and nuances, for there was not much depth and versatility required of his personality. And in those few occasions when they made love, which was performed more like a rite following steps the spontaneity was nonexistent and their passion was stale. That's exactly what had happened to her and Avik; even living out the ritual in bed had become so ritualistic that it needed not even the preamble of a kiss. The intimacy and zest that go hand in hand in a marriage lacked in Maya's. The pleasant surprises that liven up the routine and tediousness of coexistence failed to save Maya's marriage.

Aakash on the other hand, had shown a passionate side since the moment they met that had kept Maya craving for more. She could definitely imagine the possible ways in which he could make love to a woman, his unruly performance satisfying her to the core, cherishing her body making her feel like a woman. She could still hear the words resonating from his lips when he said 'to see you', and the passion that emanated from his eyes it had simply singed her. So now she felt really anxious sitting in such close proximity, thinking he could feel her uncontrollable desire for him. This warned her against herself for she no longer could remove the spell he cast on her. It would be completely hypocritical on her part to deny her soul, body and mind wanted him madly, she pondered. Maya was so deep into her thoughts she didn't realized they had arrived to her place. The auto finally stopped and their conspicuous silence was broken as he spoke. "Can you manage? Be careful when you step down. Or do you need me to come up?" He asked. "No thanks, I have a flashlight" said Maya and was about to move away when she felt a tug at her dress. Turning back she saw a lipstick lying in the now open palm of his hand. "Is this …" began Maya and was interrupted by him. "Yes, I don't think I need to treasure it anymore, it's better off with its true owner" said he and paused "… I have something else to treasure" and with this he finished and tapped the shoulder of the driver, who drove off into the night leaving Maya dumbfounded staring after him as the full meaning of his parting line dawned on her.

It was almost seven in the evening and Maya was tired to the bones, for it had been a hectic day at the college, not so much physical as it had been emotional. Today was the examination day for the first semester and she was equally tense about the tests results since they would reflect on her performance as a teacher. Coming back to her flat at the end of each day had become something endearing and comforting. Moving about in the safe haven of her small cozy flat, now practically furnished; with a cup of tea in her hand she would breathe deeply going through the day's events. As with each passing day and the subsequent changes in her life she made equal changes to the general decoration of her flat. It was somehow parallel how she had started weaving a solid pattern of life, thus rearranging her furnishing according to her life. Building her life afresh, had given her the inspiration to emulate it on her personal space. She wanted it to be clutter free with an easy flow and clean lines. For instance, she made the sitting arrangement on the floor in a traditional Japanese style –complete with mats and a very low table in the center. To this, she added an Indian touch with rugs, lampshades, and bright-colored pillows. Next to the door she placed a bust of Lord Vishnu[8] replete with thick orange garlands and a small green bulb below it for lighting during the evenings as it was accustomed in southern India. The rental furniture comprised a dinning set of a table and four chairs, a fridge, a washing machine and a TV –all rented under the careful supervision of the landlord. The rest of the things she collected from her several trips to the local markets over the month and a half that she had resided here. Although she found herself amidst her cherished new space, she felt a tug in her heart, she felt nostalgic knowing she wasn't able to share her accomplishments with her father and brother, whom she missed terribly. For a split second, she wished she could go back in time and be that carefree Maya going to high school with friends fantasizing life to be one of romance, fun and pleasures. Unfortunately, her life in Calcutta became empty with no husband, no child, no friends or family to turn to. She escaped that emptiness by abandoning what it was dear to her in search of a new opportunity: to say 'yes' to life, to love, to faith. Maya practically jumped at the sound of her cellular phone ringing to the tune of an old Hindi song from somewhere in her bag. Snapped out of her reverie, she realized that she was sitting on her bed with a bundle of tests next to her and still dressed in her work clothes. Snatching out the cellular from her bag, she saw it was Priya.

"Hello Priya!"

"Hi, so what's up? It's been ages and no word from you?" asked Priya.

"Actually I've been busy, but I was going to call you …" said Maya a little sheepishly as if excusing herself and searching for the right words. "That's ok Maya, we all are. So how's your teaching job going?" Interrupted Priya.

"Very nice, but it's equally hectic."

"How's the flat? You never invited me!" Mocked Priya.

"Really? Since when do you need an invitation to come over?" Maya snapped with equal sarcasm.

"I am joking dear! Actually I have been busy myself. I was playing hostess to my parents and Dhiraj who were in town visiting. Remember? But now they all are finally gone." Said Priya.

"So you are alone once more. How's work?" asked Maya.

"Same as usual, very tiring but hey, why not meet up and catch up?" asked Priya. "When, now?" asked Maya surprised.

"Yes! Today's Ladies Night, remember? Rita is also joining me. It will be just like before, the three of us." Priya said happily.

"Sorry dear, it's impossible today, I just got home and I have tests to correct."

"There you go again, you seem to be going back to your cocoon again." Priya said in a condescending way, which irritated Maya.

"Not really, things are different, now I have a job and a place of my own both of which need my time and attention. So I can't just go now."

"Well suit yourself; we'll meet up some other time." Priya said.

"Yes that's better, but why don't you come down to my place, this weekend?" Maya suggested. In response there was a long pause and Maya was about to interject the long silence with a repeat 'Hello' assuming there was no connection anymore, when Priya spoke.

"Say that's a great idea! If you make one." "What are you talking about? 'If I make one what? I don't follow" asked a slightly baffled Maya.

"What I mean is that we can have a housewarming party this weekend if you are a little flexible" said Priya.

"Actually, it's not a bad idea, but I would need help with it" conceded Maya.

"That's not a problem. I'll call you tomorrow and go over the details. Ok? Till tomorrow then. I'd better go now or I'll be late meeting Rita" said Priya.

"Ok, bye Priya" said Maya and hung up.

Maya couldn't get out her astonishment as she had been pondering over her lonely and quiet life in Bangalore a few minutes earlier when the universe decided to work on her favor changing all that with a phone call. She couldn't help but feel excited and intrigued with the idea of a party. All the quietness in the house would be traded for a little fun and laughter. The idea of having friends over really pleased her. How about inviting a treasured foe? Oh No! Thought she the moment his face flashed across her mind. She would not invite him, it was decided. But the sheer hypocrisy of denying what her heart missed, and whether this so-called fear of meeting him was a shield to protect her from believing what her heart already knew. If she really disliked him, why was she even considering the idea of inviting him? She reasoned. She had in internal conflict she knew as she had felt aroused being next to him yet disgusted at his arrogance.

Maya was enjoying her break in the teachers' lounge sipping coffee. The tests were all corrected and her class had fared indeed very well. Dr. Hakemi was very pleased with the results and more so with her performance as he advised her. The oral examination had also been exceptionally good. Dr. Hakemi was extremely satisfied with the overall results he was willing to give her more classes as long as he saw a replica of her first class. It was while she was meditating all these that Maryam, one of her students came to hand over the project that Maya had assigned to them the week before. Maryam was tense and asked Maya if she could give her the results. Maya was so proud of them she assured Maryam she had nothing to worry about.

"Don't worry so much dear, everybody has done well."

"Yes? Who has the highest grade, Miss Maya?" asked fluttering her mascara-caked lashes.

"Well that's a surprise, it could be you" said Maya playfully.

"Do you really mean it, Ms. Maya?" She asked now quite excited.

"Patience dear, now just go back to your class, I'll come after the break."

"Ok, Miss Maya" saying this, Maryam went away to divulge the information she got out of Maya to her friends. Maya herself was preparing to go when Ramesh, the attendant came in carrying two dozen red roses, wrapped in cellophane, along with an envelope. Maya was confused yet very surprised to see flowers, roses especially for her. So without wasting further time, she started opening the envelope when Ramesh asked in the sweetest voice "Is it your birthday madam?"

"Oh no, nothing like that …but thank you Ramesh" saying that she made another attempt at reading the note. With her heart beating as a drum she began reading the card.

I've always loved roses, especially the red ones … they say so much without saying anything. Just like you! I was dazzled by their charm, the way I feel when I am with you. Take care and enjoy the day. I'll pick you up in the evening. A.P.

"Absolutely out of the question!" She cried out as she left the roses lying on the table and headed towards her class. "Thank goodness there is no class after 4:00 p.m. today so I could leave without having to meet him." She added to her discourse en route to class. Meeting him today, certainly would not have helped matters, thus heaving a sigh of relief more like a puff she entered her classroom.

Maya came out of the bath feeling fresh and invigorated smelling like talcum and wearing her favorite sleeveless pink cotton night gown. Maya went to the kitchen to make some tea and then headed for the living room where she could sit under the dim light of the corner lamp. She turned off all the lights except the one in the kitchen creating a warm cozy glow. She decided to postpone arranging the terrace as it was getting darker and enjoy her tea indoors. Over the last few days she had been collecting nice potted plants and had put a very ethnic hanging lampshade made of cloth for the terrace light bulb. She had also bought a black clay urn and placed it in one corner filled with water, for the birds to quench their thirst and possibly enjoy a dip or two. Along with this, she had also rented two bamboo chairs and a table, which she placed on one side. Today she wanted to rearrange the pots and build a seat with a board of plywood she had found earlier, stacked away in the loft. It was wide enough to put several bricks underneath to convert it into a makeshift bench. To differentiate solitude from loneliness, Maya was learning now that enjoying solitude didn't mean being lonely. It was ironic how being in Calcutta she felt lonely even though she was surrounded by a lot of people and now finding herself alone in her flat she enjoyed solitude without feeling lonely. She also realized that just because her parents and Nikhil were far away, it didn't mean she was alone; they were still part of her life. She needed to let go of that emotional dependency on them. Living on her own had become easier as she became more introspective feeling more secure of herself letting go of fears and inhibitions. She started appreciating herself, therefore everything else around her. That's when she started noticing animals like birds, cats, dogs, cows, goats and butterflies that she had taken for granted once. A lot of these animals were alone yet they were able to survive on their own, she rationalized. She thought about the importance of having pets in one's life to soothe one's grief and fill that emptiness that humans suffer from time to time. They were indeed great companions as they loved unconditionally.

Since it was already dark outside and she had postponed the decoration for the next day, she decided then to check her guest list. Priya had called as promised and confirmed that she would take care of the food and drinks. That meant Maya had to ensure the dinner

- and after that -

service for about ten people: Priya, Dhiraj, Rita, Lalli and her husband and three or four of her students. She also thought it would be a good idea to call Maryam and Alijani and ask them to help her with the decoration. Content that she had everything almost figured out and it had not been difficult at all to manage, she was about to lay back and enjoy the remaining of her almost cold tea, when she heard footsteps on her veranda. Now who could that be? She asked herself a little startled. Possibly just the landlord going up to water the plants, but before she could rest peacefully with that thought, the steps stopped in front of her door. Feeling a little uneasy and reprimanding herself silently for not having locked the interconnecting gate, Maya began speculating the various ways of self-defense if the situation arose. Sure enough the doorbell chimed away in the quiet atmosphere of her flat. Unaware of the identity of her visitor but sure of his purpose, not coming with an intention to rob the house by ringing her bell, she asked a little boldly

"Who is it?"

"Aakash, open up"

"Oh my god," whispered Maya "What is he doing here at this time? What am I going to do?" Another chime penetrated the flat followed by a persistent demand.

"Maya are you going to let me in or do I have to find other ways?" Avoiding such a catastrophe, Maya opened the door promptly, and asked him "What are you doing here?"

"Me? Just paying a friendly visit to enquire after the roses" said he and stepped inside the flat pushing past Maya.

"Well thanks for that, but it's late now and I wasn't expecting …"

"You should have known by now that I am not so easy to avoid."

"It's really late Mr.Poorie, I think you should go now. We will meet tomorrow." "Yeah, so you still think it's very easy to shrug me off and escape, huh?" almost purred he and just extending his arms caught Maya easily. As she was a fraction of a second too late in assessing his motive, she found herself locked in his arms.

"Please, please what are you doing? Let me go!" said she struggling in vain.

"It's just that my classes got dismissed early …" Maya couldn't finish her sentence as he abruptly asked "Why didn't you call me? Why did you make me wait, and wait like an idiot?"

"I am sorry, I forgot" said she in a shaky voice and looked up to find him staring at the base of her throat where under the pressure of being held tightly by the shoulder along with her struggle, a little more than her cleavage was showing. She stopped struggling and was frozen, she kept staring at him and in the silence that followed, her heart beating loudly was something that she could not only feel but could almost hear. Aakash unperturbed and mesmerized continued to stare in silence and looked up slowly to meet her eyes and in that moment of silent intimacy they stood, stared and breathed their passion repressed till now. Their eyes communicated their individual need to be comforted, loved, and cherished and to be made love to. Both felt that deep sense of bonding, that sudden jelling of chemistry that didn't wait for introduction or persuasion. Maya felt as if time had just stopped as she was floating and watching herself from above like in an out-of-body experience. She found herself breathing harder and now she could almost hear both hearts beating simultaneously. Both acknowledged the need to be with each other and standing so closely was more like a temptation. Their eyes

- and after that -

expressed the strong urge to consummate their mutual desire pulsating in each breath they took. Unable to control their constrained passion they surrendered to their instincts.

So when he lowered his face and captured her mouth with his mouth, Maya savored the sweetness of his mouth and sensed the pulse beating on his lips and opened her scorching moist mouth to him. In reply to his lips exploring the inner, wet and slippery softness of her mouth, she bit his full lower lip, with an ardour that matched his. The smell of his after-shave, his musky odor and the remnant of a mint flavor still left behind somewhere in the inner folds of his mouth, intoxicated and drove her to madness. With a delicate but firm grip, which surprised even her she grabbed his hair at the back of his head pulling his face away from her mouth and placed it on her throat. The burning sensation from the mouth now went to her throat, where he kissed passionately as his hand started traveling from her waist up all the way to the side of her breast. Suddenly he pulled his face away from her and pulled her closer into the folds of his arm instead, and hugged her tightly. With a hand that was both gentle and strong he started caressing her head, over and over again, while with his other he held on to her tightly. Maya hugged him back with all her might without the slightest intention to let go, and started kissing his chest where the button had come undone and a pointed V of his coarse black hair was showing. She could see the hair started at the base of his throat and made a wide V as it went down all the way to his navel, as she continued opening his shirt. However, instead of letting her continue, Aakash stopped her and forced her to look at him. Maya was barely able to stand on her feet unsupported; she tried focusing on him through her passion enshrouded eyes.

"Stop it Maya, not like this!" Maya could just look at his manly face, slightly sweaty around the lips and beads of perspiration at his temples, the eyes red at the corners. But the look those eyes carried shocked and surprised her as they did not match at all with the mood of the moment, for they were steely and determined, hence she could not believe for a moment what he was saying.

"What? I don't understand ... what happened?" said Maya disappointed.

"I am sorry Maya, this is wrong ... I didn't mean to" He looked disconcerted yet embarrassed. "I thought you wanted me ... but ... wait, were you leading me on?" Maya sounded shocked but her face said otherwise, more like upset.

"Yes, I must leave now, I can't stay."

"Aakash, please don't go!" pleaded Maya.

"Don't make this more difficult than what it is Maya" and with that he practically held her away from him and started buttoning his shirt as he turned and headed towards the door. As he was opening the door she managed to catch his shirt and sobbing with tears rolling down her cheeks she made one last attempt to stop him. "No, please, don't go now, not like this!" But he gently, yet determinedly, took her hand away and kissed the tips of her fingers and went away closing the door leaving Maya behind with tears streaming down her face and a button of his shirt in her clenched palm. She was humiliated at the entire scene, at being forced to stop midway and so unceremoniously. "How dared he!" screamed Maya.

The party was in full swing and most of her guests that had come were scattered all over the terrace, with the exception of Lalli and her husband who had called to let her know they were on their way. She had finally managed to set up the makeshift bench with the plywood board, complete with couple of extra chairs and potted plants, all placed cleverly. Most of them had their drinks in their hands and with the help of Maryam and Rita, Maya had made two kinds of hors d'oeuvres as an accompaniment. While Priya catered to the rest of the eateries, Dhiraj had very thoughtfully brought along his Sony music system, which was currently belting out some weird trance sequence. However, as Maya had already found out that she would not have to stand it for long, given the frequent interjection of changing CDs and hopping from one genre to another, from pop to rock to trance to Persian music to utter confusion, she did not object to it. Hustling and bustling about the place, taking care of the guests and preparing drinks had left her no time to feel the agony of her embarrassment still eating her away. Just the trouble of organizing the party had kept her active and distracted from her disastrous rendezvous. She was so distraught after the incident she couldn't face her students or anybody at the college the next day —she literally took to bed and stayed there till the next afternoon; the only call she made was to the college informing of her inability to be present— unable to pretend she was unaffected. So the pretext of running about the place looking all excited and gregarious was a good way of deceiving herself and the others. Lost in her thoughts, she was heading to the terrace once more with a tray of fresh food when Alijani, one of her students called for her attention.

"Come Miss Maya, I take the tray you go dance."

"Oh no, thanks! I am no good at dancing and don't say 'I take the tray you go dance,' instead say let me take the tray, and would you like to dance?"

"I forgot, sorry! You need a partner Miss Maya?" he said smiling.

"Say: Do you need a partner?" said Maya, "... and I would say no, thank you." But before the lesson was over there was a great noise followed by long and insistent ringing of the doorbell. Maya excused herself and went to answer the doorbell. At the door, she found her remaining batch of students pouring in, along with others that they had brought along. Together they created a new episode, nearly all Persians both men and women wearing vibrant-colored clothes, as they came and conquered her flat and filled her heart with great joy. The once empty and gaping solitary rooms came alive with their presence as they went about leaving their mark all over. They did not want to trouble Maya with the extra heads they brought, hence they got home- cooked Persian delicacies along with their music, and of course, the deadly deceptive, potent and sweet vodka-based drink, Aarakh. Their Gorma-sabji, Taadi, and Ashe Reste, Kabab Kobide, Koko Sabji, Zereshk Polo Ba Morgh were the many delicacies that turned out to be pure gastronomical delights. This was compounded with the strong and cloying smell of their perfumes that lingered all across the rooms. It brought her immense joy when they invaded her space which she readily relinquished. Amidst all that, Lalli's laughter, which was the loudest and her appreciation of Maya's flat the most vocal announced her arrival. She came with Mohammed, and another one of her students along with her quota of drinks and a medium-sized basket covered with a pink towel that almost wriggled and bounced as if with a life of its own.

"Maya something for you" said Lalli catching her looking at the basket.

"For me! Well what is it? Don't tell me ..." but she didn't complete the sentence because at that moment the towel fell to one side and she could see a most anxious and inquisitive pair of glistening black eyes looking at her. Maya quickly uncovered it and lifted up what turned out to be a Dalmatian puppy, with small black dots all over and a tail the size of its entire length.

"Ooooh … Lalli, thanks so much, he's so cute and handsome" saying this she kissed Lalli on the cheeks.

"Wow! Thanks really both of you" thus including Mohammed, seeing how he was beaming. Naturally, all these commotion had drawn the rest of the party to the front and the puppy found a home in each set of hands. It was soon decided that today was the most auspicious day to name the pup. As expected Alijani took it upon himself to fulfill this responsibility and gave the pup its name. Thus, it was with great amusement and under lot of attention that the pup found itself addressed as Shooka, which in Persian means cheetah. So as the duck takes to water, so did Shooka, the puppy take to its name; like a miniature miracle he lapped up all the milk, the adulations and the various 'oohs and aahs!' that followed as a natural course of action. After a while when the euphoria had somewhat subsided and everyone was back to the party mood, Ali in the most solicitous manner shouted in Persian to Erfan, her most good-looking student of all, to take her out to dance. This kind of behavior was the most expected from Ali, as he was big, strong and protective like a momma bear always by her side, offering help and assistance anywhere and anytime. Even today he and Maryam had fixed the terrace and taken care of the final touches. The enormity of his belt commanded respect so at a single beckoning from him Erfan came running. Naturally cheered, clapped and prodded on by the rest of her friends and students, Maya had no option but to dance and thankfully within a short time the two-some changed to a ring of Persian young adults swishing, gliding, clapping and revolving bodies of fun, and laughter, darkly silhouetted against the terrace wall. Soon the others joined in and what started as an unavoidable chore for her became a moment of unparalleled joy. Hence, like marionettes they went on dancing, sometimes with the same partner sometimes changing as part of the dancing ring that they had formed true to their traditional way of dancing. Maya found to her pleasure that she was quickly picking up their steps and rhythm. The strenuous exercise followed by drinking with abandon made her feel as if she were on a stage, where one part of her was dancing and drinking and the other stood guard on all of her actions, thus maintaining a balance that kept her unconsciously aware of the people around her. It was then followed by a slow creeping desire to break free completely: free from her past, free from set notions, from the rigidity of her mind over herself, without the narrowness of bias, and judgmental way of thinking.

It was almost an hour later that they found themselves reclining and reposing in different parts of the flat to rest their tired feet. Another half-hour later, a messenger came for Maya carrying a huge bouquet of orchids, a small packet and an envelope. Maya was still in the terrace with her new-found joy, Shooka admiring and baby-talking to him. There was a nice breeze blowing gently moving the plants and swishing the lamp of the terrace. Priya came up with the messenger in tow, smiling mysteriously and trying hard to maintain the basic decorum of polite disinterest —but not succeeding very well— which did not go unnoticed by Maya. She came forward and signing and tipping off the messenger she made an effort at reading the note to identify the sender even though in her heart of heart she knew, which the note also confirmed.

Hello Maya, I am sorry, but not for what I did in your flat when I was there last; I am never sorry for my actions as I don't do anything that is in disagreement with my taste, and better judgment. Only this time was an exception, as my actions did not agree with my judgment. Such lapses are not acceptable, even by me, hence the apology.

Yours truly,

Aakash

Maya felt a sea of emotions all clamoring to surface and the conflict issuing thereof to keep them under control and away from the perceptive glances of Priya, who turned Maya towards her and asked her to explain the flowers.

"So what's up missy, flowers and stuff?" asked Priya.

"What's up, nothing!" said Maya indignantly.

"Nothing? Who's the guy? Tell me or I'll read the note" saying this she made an attempt at snatching it from her when Maya blurted it out abruptly.

"It's Aakash."

"Him, Maya, of all men, can you handle him?" Dhiraj who was quietly listening to all these and seeing Maya's discomfort, he interrupted Priya saying somewhat defensively, "Why not Priya? You are making him out to be some kind of demon! From what I know of him, he's a cool guy … clean-cut, responsible, and a little serious maybe, but right for Maya."

"Yeah, but a little too serious for her and I think she needs a more outgoing guy." "Really I see no point in the conversation …" said Maya.

"No? Even after the flowers and what's that in the box? Let's see!" probed Priya.

"Let her open it later, in privacy" Rita intervened who had come in the meantime and was quietly watching. Defensive about the whole thing Maya said "Oh, there's nothing like that, I'll open it right away!" and taking off the tape she ripped apart the wrapper indiscriminately and out came a small velvet box. Nestled in the cottony fold lay a small brooch of fine craftsmanship and suitably expensive —a ladybird made of gold with red wings, polka-dotted in black and two gleaming eyes of emerald— as proclaimed by Priya after seeing the make. Maya was left gaping at it and admiring it in such a way that the array of her emotions lay exposed to all. The remnants of the party became a haze for Maya: a sequence of meaningless events, where everything went clock-wise till the moment the house was warmed, guests happy and satiated, evening enjoyed and extended till the crack of dawn and Maya almost delirious with laughter, fun, and a general overdose of everything. The flowers, gifts and the note added that extra zing in her life, which seemed promising and full of activity and encounters in the near future.

Days and weeks had passed and Maya's life seemed to have formed a new pattern of its own but refused to let go of some behaviors. The only exception to this was the ever new adventures of Shooka that was growing up like a weed, and the only respite for her not to get caught in the mundane routine of life. From the time she would come back home till the moment before setting out for work, Shooka was the life and source of all activity occupying great part of her time; that apart, she was very much the same woman with same fears and insecurities still hurting after the last encounter with Aakash. So when Priya came to her flat on a Sunday to inform that her wedding was getting registered next month, in the presence of family and a small gathering of friends, Maya was very happy. So life was not such a drab after all, not just an array of things to be done at given times, in a certain way and expecting a fixed outcome; there were occasions that breached the monotony of it all.

"Congrats Priya, I'm so happy for you that you have not postponed it further" said Maya.

"Yes, enough of this courtship, it's time for me to get settled. Let's see if I am lucky this time" agreed Priya smiling.

"Of course you will be, and why not? That guy was a creep and whatever happened was for the best. Besides, Dhiraj is a nice and fun to be with guy. I think both of you will do great together" concluded Maya wisely.

"I hope you're right Maya. Anyway, I want you to take off that day, because the ceremony will be at 3:00 p.m. at the Iyer Hall near my place. Don't do the disappearing act like last time. Ok?"

"Ok dear, I'll manage something" said Maya.

"God I am feeling so tired and lazy …" and saying that Priya lay back on the bed and stretched her arms above her head. "… I simply don't feel like rushing back" said she and spotting the jewelry box still lying in the corner of the table amidst a pile of books she asked "So what's going on with you and Aakash?"

"Nothing much actually," said Maya feeling the disappointment creeping in her voice, "haven't seen him for a long time."

"You mean much ado about nothing? Not even a phone call?" asked Priya a little incredulously.

"No, we have been in touch that way, but no meeting. Maybe he's still not back?" pondered Maya.

"Back? Where did he go?" asked Priya.

"Well, he's in Delhi on a business trip since last week" said Maya.

"Maybe he's back and taking it easy? Well, that's what I wanted to warn you about. Aakash is not the type who would take you out and do things to make you happy and keep you engaged. He would rather do things to entertain himself; he's not someone you need for sure. A nice, easygoing, cheerful guy who will take you out and spend quality time with you is the one for you; not someone who just sends pompous and weird notes and orchids! Imagine not roses, but orchids. I am surprised he didn't send you cacti. I'm sorry to tell you this, but that's how I feel" said Priya gesticulating each word to further emphasize her point, the gravity of Maya's mistake and the unsuitability of Aakash as her life partner.

"Well, he did send roses, once" said Maya meekly. However, each of Priya's words had found its intended mark on Maya's heart as she unconsciously agreed with the logic Priya was putting forward. Not that she agreed to her portrayal of Aakash as a pompous and self-centered man, but to the concept of spending quality time together. So she sat in silence, when Priya said "Is that enough?" I would certainly not date a man like that. In fact I would teach him a thing or two for taking me for granted. Simply show him the door." Maya felt like crying at her inadequacy to bring out the romance in him, which she was sure lay somewhere locked in his heart, and simply said "What can I do Priya? I am not you."

Priya in response just gave her a dirty look and said "What do you mean by that? A lot can be done! You can have a straight talk about the things you want out of the relationship, and if he doesn't comply then simply dump him and look for a better guy. By the way, he's also invited to the wedding, so you will get to see him then." Looking at her watch Priya jumped up exclaiming "Look at the time! I'd better go" and without wasting anymore time she picked up her bag and kissing Maya on her cheeks went away. Maya closed the door and came back in and sat on the bed once again, for the conversation still lingered on her mind and she could not help but wonder what it is about women and their fascination for exhibitionism in romance. What is it about flowers that always captivate women? Why is the flicker of a candle in a candlelit dinner considered the harbinger of love? Since the beginning of time a suitor in love who wanted to make his love known resorted to poetry, flowers, jewelry, display of bravery, display of wealth or any other thing that propelled him to do without following a pattern. So how in the course of time did it get caught in the compulsion of a prototype? She could come up with no answer that satisfied her logic or pacified her heart. Was Priya right after all? Things have changed and so have love and ways of courtship. She wanted to accept her reasoning, yet deep down in her heart she knew Aakash was different, thus he could be the man for her. Although she still felt abandoned and dejected she wished for Aakash to shower her with attentions –complete with flowers, poetry, and music and candlelit dinner.

Full with questions and desires of an unrequited heart she decided to write a letter to Nikhil instead, and realized that almost a year had lapsed since her last letter to him. Feeling highly emotional and desirous to talk, she began her poignant letter.

My dearest Nikhil,

It has been almost a year since I last wrote to you. I could apologize for the lapse, but I won't; for this has given me a rare opportunity to look at myself and you in a very different and unique way. To express myself better I can tell you 'Absence makes the heart grow fonder' as the old adage goes. I have realized this in its true sense as your absence has dug a hole in my heart. In the past year and a half I have had time to reflect on our childhood, which has redefined my perspective and love for you. What then appeared to be an unbearable nuisance to be easily traded for a sister or a better behaved brother, now seems like a blessing that God bestowed on me –while I was shrouded in the ignorance of my ingratitude.

Just the other day while browsing in Crosswords, the bookstore on M.G.Road, I came across the Gitanjali[9] translated into English and I simply could not resist the urge of making it a part of my life in Bangalore. As I stood there, I took a trip down memory lane as the songs that I used to sing in the seclusion of our Shymbazzar house with the accompaniment of the harmonium[10] under the strict vigilance of my tutor seemed to beckon at me. As I read the poems surrounded by shelves full of rows and rows of books the songs seemed to have all the answers I was seeking. The poems along the subsequent feelings rising thereof, of those songs during my adolescence, transformed into a deeper meaning. I paid the paltry sum of 395 Rupees for such an immense treasure and rushed home. It was a quiet Friday evening, so I took advantage and indulged in the pages of Rabindranath Tagore and my tryst with poetry began. Soon enough I was ensnared in deep thoughts and realizations amidst the strong and mild emotions that kept me enthralled as I saw myself with less pity and more love and compassion. So for once, I started to

[9]Gitanjali is a collection of 103 English poems, largely translations by the Bengali poet Rabindranath Tagore.

[10]An organ-like keyboard instrument with small metal reeds and a pair of bellows operated by the player's feet.

see that what had happened to me was a mere mishap and not some inescapable misfortune of epic proportion.

The death of a relationship is nothing but the beginning of another one. I have also started believing in a higher power, well, I always believed in God and religion as part of our Indian legacy, but it is here and now that I have fully felt His presence in life and especially in mine. Hence with that knowledge I am not compelled to look for in the confines of the temples, photos, rituals and worship. But I still love to sit in front of his picture and meditate, not as a dichotomy but as a way to calm my inner self after a busy day and center myself better.

Here in Bangalore I have noticed a very beautiful ritual that is still being practiced, unlike in Calcutta: that is the making of Rangoli — patterns on the floor with multi colored powder— in front of one's door every morning without fail. This is a custom that we are not unaware of, Nikhil. I am happy here because I am amidst people who are nice, reserved but helpful. The elderly couple that I have as landlord has taken it upon themselves to mother me. We have become very close and they know everything about me. Needless to say they are eager to meet you and Neeta and my sweet little niece Nidhi. I also want to share my new life with you. My initial weeks with Priya have done me a world of good. Priya, my friend from my University days, the one you had a terrible crush on, is getting married soon to a nice guy. She is so positive and strong that she has inspired me to move on with my life instead of dwelling on the past. You can be happy, for your sister no longer blames anyone for her misery, not even Avik and herself for that matter; for she has learned that life balances itself with doses of pain and pleasure alternatively. I sadly or fortunately belong to this group of people who has to learn from their own experiences. I needed to go through this in order to better know myself, as better phrased by Socrates, 'know thy self'. So I am now trying to take small steps every day to see that bigger picture. Well I don't want to take the full credit for being this insightful and owner of such thought process, for then I shall be indulging in half truths. My perspective in life has been reached with a certain amount of help from living my days, each day at a time –with the good and the bad ones.

Just one last word of wisdom from your didi:

Life is not what it seems! Sometimes it is quite predictable and sometimes quite the reverse, but never the same, at every stage of our lives. It's our folly that we think it to be and hence try to coerce it to give a definite shape, look and direction to it, in tandem with our vision, expectation and an underlying strong desire to play God.

Lovingly your,

Didi

As usual Maya got delayed at the college attending to her class affairs, consequently arriving at the hall at 3:30 p.m. Feeling a little guilty, yet excited with the prospect of meeting Aakash, she climbed the flight of stairs and into the hall amidst all who were assembled there. She was anxious and apprehensive. She felt like a fool for feeling this way, for it was not her marriage but her friend's. Was she not angry with Aakash, for not meeting her since that humiliating rendezvous at her place? Maya thought as she entered as quietly as possible not to draw attention. She directed her glace towards the center where some formalities were still in progress by the registrar in the presence of respective parents. Priya and Dhiraj seated among them looked very happy. Priya really looked beautiful, especially in the light pink crepe chiffon that she was wearing with a matching set of diamond jewelry. Dhiraj likewise was in a gorgeous maroon Punjabi suit with a long scarf draped around his shoulders in beige. Both of their parents were beaming and watching the whole process with an expression only to be found on the faces of proud parents. Maya decided to get closer to the couple making sure her presence was acknowledged by them and their respective parents without interrupting the proceedings. She decided to look around and spotted Rita not far from her, talking to a group of people. Not sure whether to go across and join them, she was still standing somewhat confused when she was addressed from behind.

"So here you are, late but looking more beautiful than ever, enough to excuse the lack of punctuality. I take it you are waiting for me?" Maya turned quickly to face Aakash standing behind and looking strikingly handsome in a grey suit. His unruly hair nicely jelled and combed back made him look smooth and his beautiful smile that complemented his clean shaven face tickled Maya's heart. So happy she was to see him suddenly and after so long, that she forgot that she was angry with him. Her momentary amnesia erased the enormous humiliation she felt when he left her standing at her doorstep, almost ruthlessly. Instead she blushed and thanked him. "Thanks, even you are looking different today …" she whispered and added "… and a correction is needed here, for I was not looking for you."

"As you say, but tell me dear, am I just looking different and nothing more?" insisted Aakash. Smiling a little and turning her face away from him as if to hide her feelings she complimented him. "And very attractive."

"And?" He questioned further. "Good looking! Happy?" Maya said almost clenching her teeth. "I guess I was wrong" Maya said in a very soft voice.

"What?" "Did you say something" Inquired Aakash.

"Oh, no nothing" said Maya putting her hand delicately over her mouth as if she were retracting her words. While they carried on with their flirtatious dialogue, the formalities were being completed, and there was a loud cheer from the guests. Turning towards it Maya saw both Priya and Dhiraj were being congratulated with kisses, handshakes and gifts by all present: friends, family and colleagues. Wishing to do the same, Maya headed towards them and after kissing Priya and congratulating them both she handed over her present.

"Thanks, I am so happy that you are here" said Priya.

"Well I am excited to be in the presence of the happiest and best looking couple" said Maya laughing delightedly.

"Say Priya, you never mentioned your friend could look so beautiful?" Said Dhiraj teasing them.

"Of course she can, when she is happy and dresses well like today." Said Priya.

"Oh come on now, you are going to make me blush!" Maya said awkwardly getting highly conscious of her looks, yet happy with the attention. At that moment Dhiraj said undauntedly "Come, let me introduce you to my brother, he is as reserved as you are, and in dire need of the company of good looking women" saying this he grabbed her arm and pulled her to meet his brother.

"Bro, meet Maya, Priya's best friend and Maya, this is Devendra" He said with a big smile on his face and then added with a devilish tone "Maya is a nice girl."

"Hi, nice to meet you" said Devendra extending his arm.

"Nice to meet you too Davendra" said Maya sheepishly. At that moment Maya felt being pushed aside ever so gently, and Aakash shook the hand of a slightly surprised Devendra.

"Hi, we met before" barged in with his deep voice. Devendra with a curious expression on his face looked once at Maya and then said "Sure and we also spoke at length about the NGOs. So how is it going? We never met after that day."

"Things are fine, I have been busy producing my documentary, in fact, I came back recently from the hills." said Aakash proudly.

"Where, Kashmir by any chance?" asked Devendra, still looking curiously at Maya, who was pretending to look in another direction.

"No but close to it. Actually I went to Uttaranchal. What about you, any new books?" "Actually yes, but why don't we finish this conversation later? Let's meet and catch up some day. Why bore the ladies here." Concluded Devendra looking at Maya who was indeed feeling left out and uncomfortable. Hearing Devendra referring to her, Maya quickly said "That's alright; I was going to talk to Priya anyways."

Fortunately for Maya, Rita who had just spotted her waved and approached her.

"Hi Maya how are you? Haven't seen you since your housewarming party said Rita. "Hi Rita, I am fine but what about you?" Maya said with a sigh of relief moving away from the guys.

"Well …" said Rita shrugging her shoulders "… things have been really bad for me." "Why, what happened? And where is Gaurav?"

"Well, he is the bad thing that happened to me. Let's not talk about him, at least not today." said Rita who tried to conceal her pain but was unsuccessful. Maya was deeply touched and truly sympathized with Rita since she too had experience a broken heart. Maya searched for the right words to console her friend but decided that silence would be best, and touched her instead.

"Priya hasn't said anything to you either?" She asked.

"No, actually you are the first person to do so. If I had known I would have certainly called you up" said Maya.

"Anyway, why talk about it today? Let's enjoy the party! Some things are better when they end." Rita added almost self-assured. "Don't they look great? In fact, you too look gorgeous. Nice sari, must be from Calcutta, right?" Smiling a little Maya said "actually yes, enough of experimentation with Bangalore variety." While they stood talking surrounded by people, Aakash from afar could see Maya looking exceptionally beautiful standing next to Rita. Was she always so wonderful to look at, he wondered. Whatever it was he knew she looked stunning for he was aware of the stares she got from the men around her. He was beginning to feel concerned and ridiculously jealous. More than twice he had to shrug off Devendra since he was evidently charmed with Maya, his Maya that is!

Looking at his watch he was surprised to see that it was already 7:00 p.m. and wanting to waste no time, he decided to ask Maya to finish off with all the senseless small talks and head home with him. Ever since he left her standing in her flat after the short and heated interlude, he had been very disturbed to say the least. He felt tormented that he had unwittingly hurt his dear Maya. Up on the hills he had realized the importance of her presence in his life and had almost taken an oath to make her his; by making her his wife. Subsequently, he had found the need to keep this desire under wraps, to protect himself more than Maya. He was sure now that Maya felt the same way, but he needed to confirm her feelings for him. He knew Maya was special and came into his life for a reason. This was the second opportunity he was getting at being happy and was not going to let it escape. It had been too painful to forget Sheila, too hard to learn to love again. He reflected for a moment, and realized if he wanted to start right he needed to divulge his past to Maya. He would also explain his sudden exit at her flat and his appalling behavior that cause her so much grief –and the reasoning behind it. He might also tell her how in his mind's eye he had planned out the first night of their union to the last detail. He would explain that to Maya so that she understood the motive behind the sudden termination of what could have been a passionate escapade.

Though not a very conventional man, believing in the ornamental aspect of marriage replete with an abundant display of wealth, and power; he had certain expectations of spending the first night together. He believed with all his heart, beginning the journey of a life together —of a physical, mental, emotional and spiritual kind — required a certain amount of romance, desire and passion. It also required no reservations –being able to enjoy fully the essence of one another. That is the reason he retrained himself that night, he convinced himself as he went on thinking. So even in the heat of the moment, in his emotionally and physically charged state, with his intellect and the reasoning power momentarily laid aside; he still managed to control the situation by not letting his emotions rule him but his reasoning when he found himself wrapped around Maya's arms. It would have not been fair to Maya and she would agree too. While he stood justifying his stifled emotion and reveling in the pleasure of soon being with Maya, she looked away from the group of people she was with and looked straight at him. It was a look that was understood by both as 'I am looking for you, for I want to be with you.' and it had the power to pull them towards each other ignoring the world around them. Maya didn't even realize when he approached her and holding her by the wrist he pulled her towards him. "Are you quite finished here? We can make a move then." he asked. "Yes, but I can't go with you." said Maya.

"And why is that?" he asked.

"Because I said 'Yes' to Devendra …" began Maya.

"Well, that's too bad because you are coming with me to my place" said Aakash unperturbed.

"What! Of course not! It's late as it is, and you stay away from me" said Maya incredulously.

"I did not ask you Maya, to come with me. I said that you are, and it's final. So finish your good-byes and let's go. I have a few things to tell you" said he stubbornly.

"You have some nerve Aakash after what you did to me! I'd better go with Devendra." Maya said firmly without moving.

"Maya don't make me take you by force" Maya's expression changed as she heard that because she feared a scene. Seeing Maya still unsure and adamant, he gently pulled her closer and said "You are coming with me, whether you like it or not."

"And why is that?" asked she trying to loosen the grip.

"Because I want you, need you and love you, and if you continue being adamant …" he paused "…then I will publicly announce it here and right now lift you in my arms and kiss you like you have never been kissed before. That's why" said Aakash almost menacingly. Maya stared on, shocked at Aakash's sudden burst of honesty, yet she couldn't help finding it romantic. Convinced of his sufficient willpower to carry on with the threat, she decided it would be in her best interest to head out with him. So just giving him a dirty and severe glance as she could manage she went dutifully to do as he asked her. About half-hour later and seated beside him in the close confines of the car, Maya felt afraid and highly uncomfortable. Being in the midst of people and showing anger was a different matter and now thrown together in this close proximity, she felt bereft of all her confidence. Moreover, his statement-cum-confession came as a shock to her; for she found it hard to believe that this man, who seemed so aloof could be in love. He could be caring and protective, and highly passionate, which he'd shown her on many other occasions and particularly on that eventful evening at her place; but to actually love her? Again she was sure whatever love he said he had for her would dissipate once she told him of her past. A straight-forward guy with a clean record of life minus women, how could he possibly care to make her, his part of life? So instead of letting that momentary bout of happiness that was slowly seeping out of her heart to flood her eventually, she decided to nip it in the bud, for she could not be deceived and cheated out of love again. Aakash not happy with a mute Maya sitting next to him asked "So how do you like my car?" Maya's thoughts broken by his question, she noticed that she had never seen him driving a car. So he must have bought it recently, she thought.

"Congratulations if it's a new one."

"Of course it is, and I bought it especially for you." He couldn't help but feel a little irritated with her, for he wanted to see her happy not indifferent. So he said "Do you like it, or not?"

"Really Aakash, I don't understand you at all!"

"That I am sure of ... even after that evening in your flat, you are still saying this? I thought my behavior was proof enough, and would help you to understand me and what I feel for you." Maya about to give a rejoinder decided against it for she knew that she would be unable to express her doubts about his love as had been displayed at her home, which she felt to be more of a mere physical attraction and less of the emotional kind. Hence she just gave him a stare and turned her face away from him and looked out the window. However, she did not have to continue with such detachment for too long because in a short while they were at his flat and this time totally alone.

Looking around the place she could almost relive that eventful evening when she ended up here after their outing at Soirée. Her train of thought was interrupted when Aakash came to her and holding her by the hand guided her to the sofa. Going near the entertaining center, he chose a few CDs and put them in the CD player. The familiar music flooded the whole place and her mind, which she was sure she had heard before but could not identify. He then approached her and opening the palm of his hand showed her the pieces of the note he had left for her that morning and she in turn shredded to pieces before she left.

"I have treasured it, as it reminded me of the morning when you slept on my bed and I sat next to you looking at you and enjoying ..."

"How could you ..." began Maya getting up from the sofa highly agitated "...take advantage of me when I was most helpless, when I was sleeping?" In response, Aakash got up himself and pulled her in the circle of his arms in his characteristic way and said "Advantage, Maya? Do you know what you are saying? What does that mean to you? Most likely you don't know! If I wanted to really take advantage of you I would have had you in your flat the other day, when I had the chance and your consent to do so. If I wanted I could have done more than just kiss you. I could have had you Maya, made you totally and forever mine. Do you understand that?" said he shaking her by the shoulders.

"So what stopped you?" she mocked and deliberately refused to look at him.

"Are you blind Maya? My love for you! You spoiled child, love stopped me … I realized up in the mountains that it's not an interest that I have for, nor is it intrigue drawing me towards you and making me possessive about you, but love. It is my love that wants to take care of you and build a life with you. To treasure and cherish you, not just to satisfy my ego or quench my lust. When will you understand that Maya, when?" In a shaky voice as a result of the tears of happiness choking her she finally managed to say she did know it but wasn't sure.

"I do, but I had to be sure of it, that you are indeed in love with me and it's not a part of my conspiratorial mind playing with my imagination … and … I wanted to hear it from your lips."

"Why these tears then, and no smile playing at the corners of your mouth, to lighten and gladden my heart?" He said flicking a tear away from her cheek and then pulling her down once again beside him on the sofa.

"Because …" she paused, "… I am scared of being happy again, afraid of what you are thinking of me and hearing my truth may not be what you want to hear" Saying this she turned away from him.

"Maya ..." said he and turned her face back towards him "... look at me. What may not be true? That you love me too, that you are a nice, loving and sweet woman? A child-woman if there is one, who is happy with the happiness of others and sees the best in them? A woman who trusts others implicitly? What is not true here, tell me?"

"Yes, you may be right in what you just said, but there is a past to me, that even I am ashamed of hate and regret with all my heart. A past that might hurt your reputation and integrity and question all your good intentions; it might make you doubt all the apparent goodness you have seen in me." Said Maya with her eyes closed, for she could not afford to see what the effect these words produced in him, if it really diminished his love for her. She could not bear to see it being extinguished in the depth of his penetrating brown eyes.

"Tell me Maya, open your eyes and face me. Tell me everything you want to, everything you need to find peace and smile once again. I want to hear it all and I will still love you as you are, I promise. I don't care and if I didn't want to hear about your past in the first place, is simply because it's your past and has nothing to do with our future together. But if it makes it easier for you then I will hear it. Just try me Maya and see I will understand it all." And like an obedient girl Maya disclosed everything –from beginning to end, the saga of her marriage in explicit detail, her trip to Bangalore and her fears and doubts. Strangely enough she felt no qualms anytime during the narration, not even about sex and the lack of it, the promises and lies, the love and its bitterness. Crying and laughing, sometimes smiling sweetly and sometimes bitterly she went on unloading to him what she kept in her heart for so long. She felt lighter as she did this. Aakash went on listening to her, patiently hearing it all. Never once questioning, never justifying or patronizing; just holding her tightly and patting her head, that lay ensconced on his chest drowning it with tears … and this went on uninterrupted long into the night. First sitting on the sofa, and then sitting very close to each other, from there into the bedroom and into the very bed she had lain before, they carried their tales and confessions.

First she narrated and he played the role of an excellent listener, and it was his turn to narrate his heartbreaking story too. She listened in wonder, pain and bewilderment, the past of Aakash Poorie as he bared it to her; introducing the Puneet Poorie that he once had been, long back and that which remained behind with his dead Sheila … far back in the past. Engrossed listening to each other's confessions they lost track of time and any inhibition that they had initially. They bonded and laid bare the inner folds of their self, mind, and the vulnerability of their emotions. Locked in each other's arms and between the bouts of kissing, they carried on their discovery of each other till sleep came in and put an end gently to the soul searching and the closeness of their heated bodies. Maya slept like she never slept before, and finally woke up to the smell of coffee. She opened her eyes to Aakash sitting on the floor by the bedside with the cup. Maya got up embarrassed and looking around, slowly took in the sequence of things that might have happened till now from the time she came in last evening. She looked at Aakash questioningly and with the suggestion of an accusation and made no effort at taking the cup. Aakash understanding what could be going on in her mind, extended the cup to her and said "Drink the coffee … I am amazed and hurt Maya that you can even think what you are thinking. It is clear that I failed to give you the confidence that you can trust me implicitly; that I want to marry you and want to spend my life with you, and not 'take advantage of you' as you said earlier." Maya felt a momentary relief, yet equally ashamed at her self for having doubted his integrity; hence wanted to make amends. But before she could think of something reasonably convincing, his cellular started ringing. Left with nothing to do except to possibly stare at him or wait for him to finish off before she could speak to him, Maya decided to head to the bathroom instead. It was while she was washing away the tearful stories from last night, and tried to camouflage her slightly swollen eyes that Aakash knocked at the door.

"Maya can you hurry up please, I have to go to the office immediately, something came up." There goes my chance at salvaging the situation, thought Maya and said "'Yes, just a minute." She came out to find Aakash already dressed, with his cellular, keys and even a matching professional look, all ready to hit the road. So out went she with him without a chance to say anything of what she intended to tell him, without having another chance at drinking the coffee that still lay on the table where she had left it. Even during the course of their journey home together she sat in utter silence. Apart from the fact that she still did not have anything befitting to say, he also seemed preoccupied with his thoughts, so she opted on not disturbing him. They remained quiet till they came to her house and he drove away after a cursory, 'Bye, take care'. He didn't even wait for her rejoinder, as she was left standing at the basement of her flat – sad and numb, feeling totally bottled up.

While she was taking her bath, the cell phone started its insistent rings. Determined not to let anything come between her and the bath she was taking, which direly needed, she let it ring and concentrated on enjoying the rest of the shower in peace. In fact, the peace factor was so high that she forgot about the phone totally. Half-hour later it rang again and she jumped up a little startled from the bed and leaving the comb, picked up the cell from the table. Seeing the home icon blinking she pressed the on button and hearing her father's voice floating out, she said "Yes father, how are you?"

"Maya dear, nothing is fine here, your ma is so sick and I am indeed very worried. I didn't want to disturb you, but you know your mother. She wants to speak to you." "Why father, what happened to her? What's wrong?" she asked worriedly.

"The doctor said its pneumonia and her overall health is so weak …." Her father's voice broke away, which really scared Maya and she said

"Let me speak to her" Maya insisted which turned out to be much worse and scary compared to speaking to her father. From the moment her mother got on the phone, she started crying and begging her to leave everything and come over to Calcutta, at least to see her if not for good, before it became too late and needless for her to do so, her mother said. Maya broke down in earnest to hear her mother speak in such fatalistic way insinuating inevitable doom, thus she promised to come down soon. Sitting on the bed and clutching the bedcover unconsciously she felt a sense of dread engulfing her … this could not be happening. How could anything happen to mother? She couldn't lose her now, never … but instead of feeling reassured, she panicked more and decided to call up the airlines without any more delay. In this state of dawning fear and helplessness, she did think of

Aakash or ask for his presence at this time of crisis. But the parting and her inability to make amends stopped her from calling him up. So she concentrated on procuring a ticket for Calcutta at the earliest, which turned out to be a difficult affair; however after several calls and sufficient pleading and groveling she managed a ticket for the next day early morning flight.

Sitting in the auto and speeding towards home through the familiar twists and turns of the many roads, lanes and by-lanes Maya tried hard not to cry. She fought hard at keeping the many memories of her togetherness and moments of discord with her ma at bay ... the laughter, tears, the many ecstasies and the pitfalls of their life together as a compact and loving unit of the Ghosal family: father, mother, she and her beloved small brother Nikhil kept clamouring for her undivided attention. She tried to control the stream of tears rolling down her cheeks but it was impossible. Just when she was beginning to get a grip on her life she could not let anything fatal happen to her ma that would wreak them all ... her mother could not abandon her now.

Sitting next to her mother after two hours, she began to feel better, for she felt that she could control the situation once again. Also by miracle her mother had almost perked up after seeing her. Maya couldn't believe her mother had even regained her appetite as she started eating an apple that Maya peeled, cut, and was putting in her mouth delicately. She was holding onto Maya with both her hands and slowly chewing the apples fed by her daughter. She was quiet and kept staring at Maya with total concentration. Sometimes her eyes were brimming up with tears rolling down her cheeks, sometimes the eyes just became too moist, yet she kept on looking at

- and after that -

the face of her daughter, unable to say anything that would narrow the gap that had come between them following her divorce. She had no words to console Maya, to sympathize with her and even cheer her up. Instead of showing solidarity with her decision she had berated Maya for opting for divorce. Lying in bed and a strain to her already burdened daughter struggling with reality, and now seated at her childish behest leaving everything behind in Bangalore. Mrs. Ghosal tried hard to think what it was that Maya was doing in Bangalore, but could not recall and felt ashamed. She now realized that neither had she been supportive of Maya in her effort at etching out some normalcy in life post divorce, nor had she bothered to find out about the job she was doing. Thank god, that at least she was sure of the fact that Maya was engaged in some job, even if she did not know the details, she thought. She would find out in detail everything about her daughter, and make it up to her, but that had to wait for later. Now she had nothing to say, to justify, and even apologize for this inconvenience to Maya. However, she noticed a change in her, for she seemed somehow stronger, calmer and more self possessed; like a woman who has undergone the rigors of different stages of life and finally reached real womanhood.

Unprepared to the duration of her stay in Calcutta, she had packed the suitcase with clothes sufficient for three to four days, but ten days had gone by and she felt little guilty for her students, because by now their second semester would have started and with a new teacher. Thank God that despite her unnerving problem at hand she had the foresight to inform Dr. Hakemi of her predicament and the need to return to Calcutta. However, strangely being in the room that had accommodated her for the last twenty-five years and sleeping in the bed almost as old, she could not identify her former self anymore and the way she used to feel, for she no longer felt the sense of peace and the comfort of the old, known and familiar boundary. As shocking as it was, she realized with finality that she no longer felt any sense of belonging here anymore. Even now and sitting in the old room of hers amidst the old and worn-out furniture, her friend for years, as she lovingly looked and touched some, was confirmed of the knowledge that while everything had remained the same and in their respective places in the room and also her life now that she was back again, something fine and vital was missing. That something was her feeling of attachment and the comforts of belonging in Calcutta that was not here with her today. She could not re-connect to those old memories of her yester years spent here; neither could she generate that feeling to be at peace with herself. By going away to Bangalore she had also moved away mentally, emotionally and spiritually towards her new path of life. The transition from the Ghosal- Sanyal- back again being just Maya had totally uprooted her from all old associations, mental or otherwise and in the span of one year, Isro Layout had become her home … a home away from home. Spending these ten days had been therefore a revelation to her in many ways. Nurturing and tending to her mother's needs and being by her father's side, she could feel a little of the old Maya, answering the call of the moment, which apart she felt no other link, with them, or with any situation here; and that's when, she started longing in earnest, to go back to Bangalore, and possibly for good.

Aakash realized in the span of two days that giving time to Maya to make her understand the depth of his feeling for her and his serious intentions was a mistake; for he found it increasingly difficult to stay away from her. During this time, neither of them had called the other and the silence was turning oppressive, and almost driving him crazy. Returning to the flat that day after his sudden trip to the office; he felt a great sense of loss and missed her presence deeply. In fact he was shocked at the intensity of his anguish for her, that for a moment he thought he smelled and felt her presence in the room. He even sat on the exact same place where she had slept on, and touched the the pillow where her head lay, lovingly. He had also touched the edge of the cup where the slightly condensed impression of her lips was still visible off her mark. It was then that he had decided that enough was enough and speed-dialed her number ... but it had gone unanswered, once, twice, thrice ... with always the same droning of the recorded 'the number you have dialed is switched off, please try again later. Thank you'. Subsequently, he made up several possibilities to the message hitting his ear every time he called: her battery was not charged, but then it seemed so improbable that on a weekday she wouldn't charge her cell phone, thus he quickly jumped to the other possibility, it was stolen and therefore switched off. But not being happy with either possibility he decided to go over to her place in the evening. So he happily used this idea of going over to meet her as a good way of cooling his over-worked mind working itself up to frenzy. How could he be so stupid? He thought shaking his head and having a trace of a smile creep out at the corner of his mouth. Why did he have to drop her home in that way? Also why in the first place did he have to go to office, and not spend the day cherishing her? Why could he not take advantage of the opportunity given to him? Why? Sharp at seven in the evening, he presented himself at her doorstep; he was about to press the bell when he noticed a small note stuck to it. That's it! Thought he, she was not here and also the light on her corridor was off, for he had a small inner voice telling him that there was something wrong the moment he reached the corridor of her flat. So with a sinking heart he flicked his lighter and made an effort to read what it said, which was not much; except that she was not in Bangalore but in Calcutta and would be back after a week –some emergency. Just that! What madness was this? What cruel trick was fate playing on him? He could not bring himself to believe that Maya was indeed, not here and gone away without telling him anything, and where in Calcutta had she gone to? He had no idea. Climbing down the stairs he had a terrible urge to talk to the landlord and find out something more. But he checked himself; for he did not want to make them wonder as to his identity and intention with her ... he was not up to facing any questioning himself.

Her sudden absence from him was made unbearable by the short and precise note, that left some questions answered and many more unanswered. How in the world is he going to get in touch with her, he could not figure. Walking down and away from her place, had required quite an effort by him, considering the madness that was raging in his mind. The 'why's and 'how's' kept appearing in turns, repeatedly in his mind harassing him with such ferocity and frequency that it almost crippled his normal thinking power. Just about managing to reach his flat he went and sat on his bed and began his mental quest for her in earnest. The acute sense of loss was almost physical, this total dependency of wanting another individual with a mental and emotional crippling intensity felt new to him. Even the final parting from Sheila with her sudden and untimely death had not made him feel anything like this; for that was an end he understood, cried for, grieved over and accepted. This was different. It was despair and a huge feeling of fear associated with the individual's absence; fear, like claws pulling at his heart. He experienced an immense sense of inadequacy as a man, even as a human being at the possible prospect of loss, at his terrible pangs of loneliness … at his inability to meet her; more so at his inability to check and control his feeling; of being at the total mercy of his emotions. At this weakest side of his being, where against all his good intentions and innumerable logics and astute perceptive and clear reasoning power, he kept hankering for her mentally and craving her physically. His years of expertise, self control, education, and his mental ability to evaluate things with the consequence in mind, failed him. Thus, he lay drenched in sweat and panting on his bed from sheer mental fatigue, as he searched for a relief from this mental agony.

Smoking and stubbing the ashtray full of many cigarettes later, his thoughts focused on Priya as his sole savior. Half-hour later he fell in a deep slumber, secure with the landline number of Maya's house in Calcutta. However, this peaceful state did not last long, for when he tried calling her number the next day, he found that it was currently out of order, and remained so, adamantly for the next eight days. Finally when he was at his wits end at trying to establish a contact with Maya, and at the end of his patience and at the last vestige of his sanity, the phone started giving him a dial tone in his ears and he breathed a long sigh that started from deep down his heart and exhaled out of his mouth: the connection was restored.

Restless and unhappy as she was, Maya was moving about the place for she could not settle down completely as she had thought and as her mother expected. Instead of the span of ten days deepening the bond with her family, old house and the familiar locality, it made Maya more acutely observant of the feeling arising out of her separation from Bangalore and all its associated activities. She realized finally that moving away from her failed marriage, she had also moved away, from her roots, her past and all associations therein. She missed her flat and all things that she had left behind … when the phone started ringing. Maya could not believe the phone ringing in their living room was really their phone and not that of a neighbor's. She just did not want to get excited and then be disappointed again if it indeed was a hallucination on her part. The complaint had been lodged almost five days back and going by the standard time taken it was too soon to be ringing … hence too good to be true and her delayed response. Her father not so cynical and mother over anxious, started their individual reactions to it from the different sections of the room.

"Maya, go and pick up the phone … it's ringing" said her father.

"Yes, father" and went to see when mother put in her advisory bit.

"See who's on the phone. If it's the repairman fixing the phone, tell him to check it properly … the puja bakshish will be…."

But Maya had already crossed over and picked up the phone and said "Hello?"

"Maya is that really you?" It was the voice of Aakash across the phone, so different, so unsure and desperate.

"Aakash …" was all she could manage before she broke down.

"Maya, thank God and about time … but dear, please don't cry and make it more difficult for me. Tell me why you left without telling me anything. Don't you care for me at all dear?"

"Actually I do, and I am so sorry for coming away here without

- a n d   a f t e r   t h a t -

telling you anything... but you left me and went away …"

"What are you saying? I left you? You simply went away not telling me anything and that almost killed me." However, before she could continue further with Aakash, both her parents wanted to know who the caller was. Cupping the receiver with one hand she briefed them about his identity and tried concentrating on her conversation, in a more calm and poised way. Maya said "I'm sorry but I did not have time to inform anybody except dropping off Shooka at Priya's place. Ma was not well and I was needed here."

"Why, what happened to her?"

"Pneumonia, but she is better now almost after ten days."

"I am sorry to hear that and I can understand your mental state. Is there anything I can do?" Maya touched deeply at his concern managed to say 'thanks' before he started with his next bout of questions. Since it was good to hear his voice and know that he cared and loved her so much, she really did not mind his questions at all. But life can be cruel at times and destiny had its curious way of making its presence felt: sometimes in soothing and sometimes like now, in tumultuous way –with the phone going dead again even as they spoke. Maya simply held the now dead and silent receiver in her hand and could not believe it was really happening and not a cruel trick –sordid and cold. In the sudden silence she could have cried out and given the chance, would have run out of the house all the way to Bangalore and straight to his arms. During her stay here, she realized the need and importance of Aakash in her life. Her birth city, birth home and parents with all their memories could not match up in any way with the new life she had started living, the flat that she was slowly turning into a home. And then there was Aakash, and all that he stood for: the yet to be fulfilled promises, the attention, the concern and the protectiveness. All that which made her initially waver in her decision to stay single as long as possible and finally over a period of time accept the inevitable without struggle and of free volition; of joining her life with that of his. A decision that was reached because of as much of his persuasion to that of her own desire not to walk the path of her life solitarily, but of living out each other's dreams and hopes along with fulfilling all their needs. Now to have this sudden and abrupt end to the growing connection between them of an unsaid acceptance of each other following the realization of their unconscious dependence and the need to make it conscious.

However, with the line turning dead and Maya wrought up, she decided to head towards the telephone complaint office of their exchange in the locality. Coming back after forty-five minutes dejected, Maya entered her room and sat on her bed. At least when she had gone out she had the hope that the problem was minor and could be easily fixed, with the hope that is eternal and lighting the hearts of many despairing human beings. The tears of frustration and repressed agony rolled down her cheeks slowly and deliberately; clenching both her palms she beat upon the bed repeatedly all the while cursing her self for not being able to finish the call. She would have definitely felt better if she could tell him when she intended to go back. Aakash, an absolute manna from heaven and now the same phone dead again: conversations, clarifications and pacifications abruptly truncated; followed by the ultimate confirmation of the telecom department -Cable Fault. Her mother also shared Maya's laments and her father expressed a growing irritation. Apart from that life seemed fine enough in the Ghosal family except to Maya.

Mother was recuperating better and faster than the doctor's prediction and Nikhil was coming home to see her with both his wife and daughter. What started off as an impending doom eventually turned out to be a family reunion and a cause for celebration. Maya could not help but assign the cause and signs of early recovery to the arrival news of Nikhil and company and the general feeling of bonhomie, but this time without any trace of the old sibling rivalry. Post divorce catharsis, finding a job and growing along with it in an independent unit to call 'home' to; she not only succeeded to wipe out every trace of sibling rivalry, but had started seeing many of his quirks as less of that and more of his endearing traits and fun of the childhood years. So it was with equal happiness that she welcomed, the news and them, in person, a day later.

While things were re-arranging themselves congenially in Calcutta, things in Bangalore and in Aakash's life were also taking a course, though in a different way. Tired of waiting anymore he simply decided to go down to Calcutta and bring her back with him. But luck seem to be really evading him for no matter how hard he tried he could not get himself a reservation for a Calcutta bound domestic flight, all seemed to be miraculously full, and would be so till the next four days. Had it ever happened before to him or to anyone else, he wondered? He was sure not; helpless and dejected and at the end of his tether, decided to wait. So, while destiny dominated and crippled Aakash to a standstill, it livened up the Ghosal family in Calcutta, with a reunion of sufficient merriment and happiness. Meeting and sharing and feeling the five adults and a tiny tot found themselves bonded deeply and tightly. Food, medicine, laughter to making beds on the floor, to baby marks all over with diapers, baby food, baby smell, to stories, to the variation in behavior, mood and overall atmosphere that affected all. However, sadly Maya felt strung up like a tightly-winded puppet doing things mechanically without really feeling much. She simply counted her time and kept churning the thought of going back to Bangalore in her mind, at the earliest and meeting Aakash. And finally in one of their merriest moments she broached the topic and stuck to her guns of going back, backed by sufficient amount of strong reason and eventually managed to win.

Thus achieving initial success, she went on with the second step of booking a ticket for the next day, but unsuccessfully. She found out to her dismay that she would also have to wait the next two days for it. Still she felt better and calmer, for it was now just a matter of time. The timelessness, of not knowing, when she could go back was at least gone; so she decided to pack her luggage with more finality than she had last time. For then it was a question of running away from it all … mingling in a crowd of faces and bodies of unknown existence, almost losing her self in the indifferent sea of people- seeking shelter! Now it was another matter … now she was going back with much greater confidence, love and expectations that tends to arise from the known boundaries and known grounds; expecting after knowing what to expect, fully and totally. It would be going back home, 'home where the heart is'… to the new, yet old familiar settings of Isro layout, to her own single cot, to the small living room, to the slightly-yellowed tiled bathroom, to everything that is there and to her Shooka. Just the thought of him, brought forth a mental picture of how he would react to seeing her again after so many days … first looking with disbelief at her, whether it is indeed her, his mommy, or a mere mental projection of his mommy, followed by the dawning confirmation in his eyes and finally his jumps and barks, to land straight into the warm folds of his mommy's arms; mused she, with a smile that began at the corners of her mouth and stretched to its full length and spread all over.

Now sitting in the aircraft and floating amidst the white and nebulous clouds, she felt at peace with herself. Taking the 6:50 a.m. flight to Bangalore she had the privilege to see the still trapped rays of dawn: trapped among the clouds in some places, yet breaking free in some others with its strong and piercing yellow rays of liquid gold which came through the open window on the right side where she sat. They touched her at an angle gently caressing part of her face down the neck and the whole right hand, as a gesture of confirmation and agreement with her decision to return to her life in Bangalore. That gentle, slightly warm, sunlight in the very cold inside of the aircraft seemed ominous to her: full of promise and of intense hope for her future. Sitting high up in the sky at an altitude of 25-30 thousand feet above sea level as informed by the captain, she felt a strong and strange closeness to god, that universal and omnipresent presence, to the state of peace and hope and faith, the whiteness of being as manifested by all thing good and pure, to the enhanced state of energy- strong, powerful and elevating. She closed her eyes and felt the surge of these feelings sweeping over her and bringing a state of tranquility hitherto un-experienced. She drew in a huge breath of air, to fill up her entire lungs and take in this good feeling deep inside her and almost felt heady and ecstatic. And in that moment too surreal to be true, she felt a deep sense of contented emptiness, of a lightness of spirit- totally unburdened; and her heart swelling and surging in a feeling of such goodness and positivism which eventually led to a huge and unchained feeling of love. Love that knew no bounds, had no bounds, love that was not for anything and anyone in particular, but an all pervading feeling that began in her heart and spread all over her, her mind, her thought process and the essence of her being. Love that accelerated her heartbeat and her breath, that made tears creep slowly out of the corners of her eyes, made her wish if she could open her hands wide enough standing on a mountain top and dissolve the things around her and be part of the whole universe, the cosmos, if that was possible? Love that set her free!!!

And gradually Maya drifted down to deep slumber and remained there for a long time, and opened her eyes hours later with bewilderment and looked into the eyes of the hostess, who was shaking her and saying something, very close to her face ... waking up from that deep peaceful state to the request of the hostess to unfasten her seat belt, and join the fellow passengers as they made a beeline to the exit: Bangalore was reached.

Struggling with himself and against time, Aakash was a shadow of his otherwise calm and poised self: both emotionally and physically. The physical manifestation of his over-wrought and nervous state were many, a week long growth of beard that was no longer stubble: black and angry standing against his hollow cheeks. Black circles bespoke of sleepless nights spent by consuming innumerable cigarettes. The hair long, untidy but tied back today, all suggested the pathetic stage their owner was in; the mental turmoil, he had undergone. Just wearing a pair of jeans and a full sleeve shirt with a canvas side bag of his wear-able stock for two days, he had his left leg up on the curb stone in his effort to buckle his sandal strap. Even with an afternoon flight to take, he knew, being in the airport would help sooth his ragged nerves and acting on that thought, he was here and now, so early. It was almost 10:00 a.m. now and he had long hours yawning ahead of him to help him board the 12:25 p.m. flight to Calcutta, but that was ok, felt he, for it was like being already on the first step to Calcutta that is to his Maya and then taking the final step of bringing her back here and thereby rescuing himself from the hell that he had been living in for the last almost two weeks now. So it was with this warm and comforting thought that he was proceeding towards the entrance, inhaling huge puffs of strong nicotine through the inch long filter, of his favourite cigarette, when he stopped dead on his tracks. Has his vision become so bad that he has started hallucinating mid-morning, he asked himself aloud? How else could it be that not twenty yards away with a single trolley suitcase Maya was coming out?

Struggling with her handbag that kept coming off her shoulder and the trolley jumping on the tiled parapet, with the now stronger rays of sun on her eyes, Maya was really finding it difficult. She thought to herself that she could have done away with these small discomforts and unavoidable delays before reaching her destination: first Priya's house to pick up Shooka then straight to Aakash. Barely managing to walk straight and steady, all she concentrated was how to catch an auto and cover the necessary distance and be with him. All the peace and serenity she had experienced in the lap of the sky now seemed distant and far removed from the poignancy of the moment, but not in any way absurd and redundant. So she went on half toppling and half walking, half dragging and half lifting smack against a hard and immovable barrier, that of the chest of a man, as she jerked to a halt and looked up to see properly; that too in the arm of a man who gripped her hard and shook her once to recognition, surprise and total joy.

"Aakash" Maya's voice trembled "... what are you doing here?"

Aakash just stood there holding her in the middle of the busiest part of the airport, the entry point. Both their luggage had fallen around them in a sort of circle and they stood in the middle, totally oblivious of the curiosity they generated. Aakash with his eyes filling in with moisture just stood there impervious to what Maya was saying to him, and did not seem to see much of what was lying ahead of him, except Maya. So they just stood there in each other's arms, the only two things alive amidst everything near and around them frozen as if in time, with one thought reverberating in his mind "My Maya is here, she is here, we are together, finally ... we are together again ... my Maya and me, she's in my arms now" he could almost hear himself say this. Maya shocked and happy to meet Aakash in this unexpected way kept repeating the same question, once, twice...and by the fourth time, she realized that she was saying the same question over and over again with no response from him. That's when she looked at him properly and found the state he was in. The mental struggle that was evident in the way he looked and in the overall impression one would get looking at him. He was there, but only physically, while mentally he was miles away locked securely, such that reality could not reach him, as he remained in that daze that was beginning to alarm her. She was instantaneously full of remorse and held herself guilty of this crime of having put him through this trauma, albeit unwittingly; why had she not given a call before going? Why not even one from Calcutta, before the phone went dead? But these questions seemed totally inconsequential, now that the damage was done, still she felt sorry and ashamed with herself. She felt that if she had told him 'sorry' back at his flat and also how much she loved him, neither would have gone through so much of heartache and mental agony. Aakash had literally wrecked his body and mind worrying about her, and just looking at him she could see how he was just a shadow of the vibrant man that he used to be once, before he fell in love with her and lost all his self control and maybe even his free will. The competent and efficient man so in control that she saw and fell in love with, and this transformed man as standing before her was so different from what she had idealized and loved. Could she continue loving him and want to be part of him, of this newer, weaker man? The man who succumbed to the throes of his passion and love for a woman, that too almost at the cost of his whole existence? The man she had seen as a strong man so sure of the worldly ways and confident of his self and actions. The same man who now stood as a mere shadow of all those qualities, what had initially attracted and later made her fall in love with. The answer could have been in the years back, pre-divorce and minus that eclectic moment, of the moment of truth and realization in the aircraft flying within the clouds; but going through all that and undergoing her process of self discovery and her subsequent growth during her stay in Bangalore and building a life there, and of the love that she felt emanating from Aakash as they both stood in each other's arms could give only one reply 'YES, yes ... for umpteenth times! So without wasting anymore time, she started collecting their bags and finally putting his bag on his shoulder gave him a nudge and like magic he came out of his stupor and took away her luggage from her and with his free hand drew her closer and asked "Where shall I take you Maya, your place or mine?"

With a coquettish look and a smile twitching at the corner of her mouth all ready to break out into one big happy and contented grin, Maya looked up to his hypnotic eyes and said "Really after all this …. Do you need to ask?"

EPILOGUE

Well, that was an end to their wait from everything that was making their life away from each other, miserable and unbearable. So finally they walked away together; happily merging with the teeming humanity around them, and not into the distant horizon of eternal bliss and love or to the traditional concept 'lived happily ever after.' Instead they walked, straight to life with all its blessings and curses, to that life where they are to live as two human beings full of the qualities that make them mortals and not gods. They must live the same life amidst the countless other people who share their same aspirations with all their earthly attributes and limitations to make music out of their dreams and hopes; as they probably succeeded or perhaps they failed and those who will come after them seeking the same and managing almost the same. However, love had its unique way of making its presence felt. No amount of obstacle had ever managed to keep people from taking the plunge into love with its myriad forms and expressions; no powerful skeptic had managed to persuade humanity of the worthlessness and futility of love in the life of men; and no one ever would. Those who had been tempered in the fire of love had often emerged transformed into a completely different being, that is, a more caring individual, more humane towards his fellow brothers. Seeing love for what it was has allowed the conclusion that sometimes one's entire life was not enough to live out a life of love. Finally to realize that Love is not a song sung in the strain of one single chord, but a medley of notes and chords forever trying to bring a sense of peace and harmony out of chaos and imbalance and it is in one such moment of truth that love is experienced in its truest essence.

- and after that -